TAYLOR TAKES CHARGE

A PORTLAND COURT ADVENTURE

BY

CHARLES UTLEY

ISBN 1613648375

EAN 978-1613648377

'Taylor Takes Charge' was first published by Night Publishing who can be contacted at: http://www.nightpublishing.com.

To Anna, Isla, Zane and Peter.

Without their patience the book would never have been written.

Chapter 1

Renewal

As the cab rounded the final bend of the long drive, Ben had his first view of Portland Court Preparatory School for Boys.

It was impressive, at least from a distance. The main building was definitely the Georgian original. Amazingly, nothing had been added in Victoria's reign or later. It must, in its heyday, have been a splendid gentleman's residence. But he could tell, as the taxi got closer, that its earlier glory had become somewhat faded over the years. The present owner (he knew the headmaster had been the owner for at least thirty years) could be commended for not having committed any architectural atrocities, but it didn't look as though anyone had bothered with much in the way of routine upkeep either.

A couple of hundred yards to the left of the house was what looked like a stable block.

Sweeping down from the house to the cliffs overlooking the English Channel was what must once have been a rather splendid lawn. Now, it was a makeshift playing field, covered with mole hills.

Those would soon be trampled flat by energetic boys chasing footballs. But, for the present, the moles were in the ascendancy.

'Good luck, sir,' the taxi driver said it in a tone which suggested that luck would be needed.

Ben handed over a precious ten shilling note and was relieved to be given 7s/6d in change. With a large trunk at his feet he stood for a moment gazing up at the building. It was surprisingly quiet. The thirty boys (it was not one of the more well known and successful prep' schools) should all have arrived for the start of the new school year, but there was no sign of them. All was deathly silent.

But there was someone watching him. He knew it for certain. Who it was and where he or she might be, he had no idea. He just felt it. He looked up again at the house. He could see no one. Yet he was sure he was being studied carefully.

He bent down and heaved the heavy trunk up. Then he staggered up the steps to the front door. It was ajar and he decided not, for the moment at least, to ring the bell. He pushed the door open and walked in.

* * *

The watcher smiled. It had to be the new master. It was too early to know for certain, but the watcher felt reasonably confident. Time would tell. The watcher slipped quietly away from the window.

* * *

Ben found himself in a large hall. Ahead of him was a rather grand staircase. To his right and left were doors to what must once have been the principal reception rooms. Beyond the door on the right was a large open fireplace. No fire was burning. Neither were there any radiators. He could see that his mother had been right to insist that he brought several thick jerseys with him.

There was still no sign of life. He put the trunk on the floor and coughed loudly. Perhaps the secret watcher would appear.

A moment later, a door beyond the staircase opened and a boy of about twelve emerged.

'Good afternoon, sir. Are you Mr Glossop?' The boy smiled at the eighteen year old new master.

'Yes, how do you do?' said Ben, a little stiffly.

'Delighted to meet you, sir,' the boy thrust out his hand in greeting. 'I'm Taylor. I'm to show you round.'

Ben was immediately struck by the boy's self-confidence. Indeed, Taylor clearly had none of his own nervousness. The boy seemed to be entirely at home and very much in charge.

'I should leave your trunk there. I'll get another master to help you carry it to your room later. I'm afraid Portland doesn't run to a handyman. Sometimes I wonder what Mr Spencer does with all the fees.'

Ben, rather taken aback by Taylor's outspoken comment, could think of nothing to say.

'Would you like to follow me, sir?' Taylor turned to the stairs. 'We'll start with the masters' quarters.'

Ben dutifully followed the boy who continued to chatter happily.

'We'll just whiz round quickly, if that's all right, sir, then I'll take you to the masters' common room for the renewal meeting.'

Ben had no idea what the "renewal meeting" might be, but he thought it better not to show his ignorance.

'That sounds a jolly good idea. Lead on, Taylor.' Why, Ben wondered, was he using such language? He would never have dreamt before he got to Portland Court of saying something was a "jolly" good idea.

'The masters' rooms are on the top floor, sir, where the servants used to live. Our dorms are on the first floor, in the grand rooms. Gives a better impression to parents when they come to look round, you see. It's a bit hard on you and the other masters, but I suppose there wouldn't be jobs for you if our parents weren't impressed by the dorms.'

Ben wondered whether he ought to rebuke his guide for being so disrespectful, but there was something rather charming about the boy's openness which made it very difficult to be cross.

Taylor walked briskly along the top floor corridor, so briskly that Ben almost had to run to keep up. As they passed each door Taylor announced the name of the occupant and his job.

'Mr Rice there, sir, he's Latin, Greek and the boiler.'

'The boiler?' Ben couldn't help asking, so odd did the job description seem.

'Yes, sir, Mr Rice keeps the boiler going, for the hot water, you know. He's awfully good at it.'

They reached the end of the corridor. Taylor opened the door on the right.

'This is your room, sir. I'm afraid it's a bit cold in the winter, but it's not too bad.'

Ben glanced in (Taylor was making it clear that there was no time to go in and look around properly). It was surprisingly large for a former servant's room. It had probably housed two or three maids at one time. There was a narrow iron bed on the right, a wardrobe and chest of drawers on the left and a desk and chair under the window.

Taylor closed the door and turned to the one opposite it. 'This is Miss Wilton's room, sir. She's new too. She's the Under Matron.'

He raised his hand and knocked on the door.

'There's no need to disturb her now, Taylor,' said Ben, slightly perplexed as to why this was the only member of staff to whom the boy felt it necessary to introduce him.

'Oh, I think it's a good idea, sir.' As he spoke, the door opened and a slim blonde girl of about Ben's own age looked out.

He suddenly felt himself blushing in confusion and embarrassment as he took in her astoundingly good looks. Fortunately, the ever-confident Taylor was there to keep the conversation going.

'Good afternoon, ma'am,' he said, 'this is Mr Glossop, the new master I was telling you about.'

'How nice to meet you,' she smiled at him. 'I'm Sarah Wilton.'

Ben began to recover his composure and would have been delighted to linger for a few more minutes, but Taylor was in a hurry.

'Sorry, sir, but we've got to dash to the renewal meeting.'

Ben grinned at Sarah and rushed off after Taylor.

'Oh, by the way, sir, better not say you know it's the renewal meeting. Mr Spencer and the others all like to make it sound like a new idea. I'll explain it all later.'

They took the stairs two at a time and got back down to the hall. Taylor knocked on the door to the right of the entrance to the house. He didn't wait for an answer but opened the door and ushered Ben in.

There were six men sitting on various assorted armchairs. Ben guessed that their ages ranged from about forty to seventy. Taylor addressed the oldest, the only one Ben had met before, at the London interview.

'This is Mr Glossop, sir. I've given him a quick look round. I'll get back to the stable block now.'

So *that*, Ben realised, was where the boys were. He walked into the room.

'Excellent, Taylor, come back in fifteen minutes' said Mr Spencer. 'Come and sit down, Glossop. We were just talking about you.'

Ben sat on the edge of the chair to which the headmaster was pointing. There was silence for a moment and he used it to study his new colleagues.

It was hard to think of them as being his colleagues. They all, even the youngest, seemed so old, and they were wearing a kind of uniform. All were in tweed jackets with various rather elderly food stains on the lapels. All wore crumpled grey flannel trousers. All had dull coloured ties with even more signs of past meals adding slight colour. For a second Ben felt a twinge of pity for them. After all, this was the first day of term. You'd have thought they might at least have had their jackets and trousers cleaned in the holidays. The fact that none of them had done so spoke volumes about their home lives. There could be no loving wives waiting for these men.

'We were just saying,' said Mr Spencer, 'that we've all been getting a bit set in our ways. We think that the time has come for renewal.' He paused to let the import of his statement sink in.

A man of about sixty-five, who had given the impression of being asleep despite having a pipe clasped between his teeth, muttered his agreement. 'Exactly the right word, headmaster,' his eyes were still closed, 'renewal.'

Mr Spencer continued. 'The thing is, Glossop, the boys are an awful lot younger than we are.'

Ben could hardly disagree.

'Of course, it's our duty to help them to grow up, to age. But we must also do all we can to let them enjoy their youth while they have it. Do you agree, Glossop?'

Ben was surprised by the question. He had formed the impression that Mr Spencer had embarked on a soliloquy.

'Oh, um, yes, sir. Of course, sir.'

Mr Spencer smiled kindly at the young master. ‘No need to call me “sir”, Glossop, “headmaster” will do. But I’m glad you share my philosophy. It can be tiresome when one employs a new member of staff who doesn’t have the same progressive outlook as one has oneself. Now, where was I?’

‘Let the boys enjoy their youth.’ This was the youngest of the other masters. It seemed to Ben that he spoke with an air of impatience, almost of disapproval.

‘Ah, yes, thank you, Hempson. I know how eager you are for the boys to do that.’

Hempson scowled, just for a second, but Ben saw it.

‘The problem is,’ Mr Spencer gave no hint of having seen Hempson’s expression, ‘we elderly men, and even young Hempson, are not always that good at understanding youthful high spirits. We can be a little short with the boys when, perhaps, we ought to be more tolerant. Isn’t that right, Hempson?’ There was another brief scowl, but, again, Mr Spencer seemed oblivious. ‘That’s why we’ve been thinking of ways of achieving some sort of “renewal” for the school. And, do you know what? We think we’ve found the answer.’

The headmaster paused. Ben wasn’t sure whether he was meant to respond. He was saved from attempting a contribution by an interjection from the apparently sleeping pipe smoker.

'Indeed we have, headmaster. And the answer is sitting right there, on that very chair.' His eyes remained firmly closed, but he made a stabbing motion with his pipe in the direction of Ben.

'Exactly, Rice.' Mr Spencer beamed at Ben, 'we're all agreed, aren't we, Hempson, that salvation for Portland Court rests in the hands of young Glossop?'

Although the question, if that was what it had been, had been addressed to Mr Hempson, he was the only one, Ben noticed, who did not instantly start nodding enthusiastically.

No one spoke. It occurred to Ben that he was now expected to say something.

'Well, sir - I mean, headmaster, sir - if there's anything I can do, I will gladly do it.'

Ben immediately thought his reply had been inadequate. The problem was, though, that he hadn't got the faintest idea what Mr Spencer's proposal might be.

'Splendid chap,' the headmaster leapt to his feet, 'I told them we could rely on you. So many other young men these days would have been selfish, would never have thought of the good of the boys, would just have thought of their own interests. I salute you, Glossop. And so do we all, don't we, Hempson?'

Ben felt it wrong to remain sitting while Mr Spencer was standing and he, too, jumped up, but not before noticing another scowl cross the face of Mr Hempson who, yet again, failed to answer the headmaster's question.

'Gosh, I mean, well,' Ben was flummoxed. The difficulty, of course, was that he still hadn't any notion as to what it was to which he had agreed, but he could tell he had been very noble. 'I do hope I won't let you down, sir, I mean, headmaster.'

'I know you won't, dear boy.' Mr Spencer was beaming again. 'Taylor will explain the details.'

For the first time, Mr Rice opened his eyes. Then, very slowly, he eased himself out of his chair. Once satisfied that his circulation had coped with this obviously dramatic turn of events, he walked over to Ben and put an avuncular arm around his shoulders.

'What a splendid chap you are,' said Rice, 'I think we're going to be tremendous chums.' He pulled Ben towards the window, away from the others, and his voice fell almost to a whisper. 'There's a way I can help you, you know.'

'Oh, that's very kind of you, sir.' Ben couldn't think how else to address this venerable old man.

Mr Rice winked at him. 'It's difficult, I know, but you and I are equals. You mustn't call me "sir". I'm Rice, just another Portland Court Master, like you.' When they were out of the others' hearing,

Mr Rice continued, 'What you need, old chap, is as much experience as possible. You'll only be teaching two or three subjects here, but I dare say you'd like to try your hand at one or two others. Am I right?'

Ben could tell what answer was required. 'Yes, of course, that would be wonderful.'

'I thought so, an ambitious chap. I was sure you were. Well, we can feed that ambition. This is what I'll do for you.' He let out a sigh as though to emphasise his generosity. 'Every now and again, not every day mind you, I'll leave some of my classics prep here,' he pointed to a shelf below the window, 'and you can mark it.' He held up his hand. 'No need to thank me, it's a reward in itself just to help a young man on the threshold of life.'

Before Ben could express the gratitude which he could tell was expected of him, his right arm was grabbed by Mr Hempson, the scowler.

'Just a word of warning, Glossop,' Hempson spoke in a sort of hiss, 'never trust Taylor.'

Mr Spencer moved at a pace which astounded them all. In an instant he was beside Ben and guiding him towards the door and into the hall. He shut the door behind them, looked around as though to make sure no one could hear him and spoke urgently to

Ben.

'I don't know what Hempson said to you, but I can guess its import. Just remember that Taylor is far more important to this school than Hempson will ever be.'

The door behind the stairs opened again and Taylor appeared.

'Ah, Taylor,' said Mr Spencer, 'Mr Glossop has kindly undertaken to be duty master every day. Perhaps you could fill him in on the details.'

Mr Spencer turned, opened the door and went back into the masters' common room.

Taylor gave a sympathetic smile to Ben. 'It needn't be too bad, sir, renewal I mean,' he said.

Ben was thoroughly confused. 'What is all this about "renewal"? And what did Mr Spencer mean by saying I was going to be duty master every day?'

'Ah,' Taylor nodded sagely, 'I see it wasn't all explained. Well, what they want is for you and Miss Wilton to be in charge of us from prep until the mornings on every night.'

'That was another thing,' said Ben, 'what is "prep"? Mr Rice said something about that too.'

'That's simple, sir, "prep" is what dayboys call "homework". We can't have homework because we don't go home. Instead, we have prep. We do it every evening. You'll be in charge of it. Then you have to mark it later, if it's prep you've set, or if it's prep Mr Rice leaves out for you.' Taylor thought for a moment. 'Did you go to a day school, sir?'

'As it happens, I did.' Ben instantly thought he sounded too defensive, but he also thought it important that these privileged boys should not run away with the idea that they were in some way superior to others, just because their parents were able to pay for their education. 'State grammar schools are actually quite good.'

'Oh yes, sir,' Taylor was nodding furiously, 'I know that. They're packed with really bright kids. Not like here at all. I'd say you were really lucky, sir. And all your masters would have been to colleges, to teach them how to teach. But Portland Court's not too bad, even if some of us are a bit thick and the masters have had no training. If you don't mind me saying so, sir, I don't think you'll be completely disappointed in us.'

Poor Ben. He had decided to give Taylor a lesson in humility, only to find the tables turned. And that reference to teachers not being trained did rather strike home. After all, he was not only untrained as a teacher, but he was also only eighteen, a boy straight out of school. No grammar school would ever have dreamt of employing someone of his age as a teacher. He had been surprised when told he could get a teaching job between school and university, but the man at the agency had explained everything.

'Some of the smarter prep schools,' he had said, 'are now being a bit snooty about employing school leavers, but most still do it. Of course, it won't go on forever. The government is bound to step in soon and insist that even private schools must only engage chaps with teacher training qualifications. But that's not a worry for you.'

Ben was a little embarrassed. It was time to change the subject. 'I'm sure, Taylor, I won't be disappointed, but do tell me more about renewal.'

Taylor smiled in an understanding sort of way. 'Well, sir, it's a bit hard on you, I'm afraid. It means you and Miss Wilton will be in charge of us boys every evening. You'll never be able to go down to the village, to the pub like the rest of them. And some of the boys, especially the younger ones, can be a bit of a handful. But we can sort things out so it's not so bad. And we're quite used to it. We have renewal every year, sir. It's why Mr Spencer gets a gap year master every September. It's so the rest of them don't have to be bothered with us boys after lessons.'

Ben very much wanted not to believe Taylor, but only a moment's reflection led him to conclude that the boy was almost certainly right.

'Anyway, sir,' Taylor continued in a business like tone, 'we need to get one or two things straight. First, sorry to ask, sir, but are you a great believer in whacking?'

Ben was about to protest at the boy's forwardness but, yet again, something stopped him from doing so.

'Well, I think it can occasionally be beneficial, but only as a last resort.'

Taylor grinned. 'Thank goodness, sir. Last year we had a gap year master who thought whacking was the most important part of the job. Renewal was a complete disaster. We even got round to planning a mass escape. We were going to steal a boat and sail away. We collected all sorts of things we would need. You know, air rifles, fishing rods, old blankets, bits of grub. But it was all right in the end. Mr Staughton, that was the renewal master, left under a cloud.' The boy changed the subject. 'Miss Wilton's a real looker, isn't she, sir?'

This time Ben did manage to express his disapproval. 'Really, Taylor, that is no way to speak of a lady.'

'Sorry, sir, it's just that my Pater always says that it's polite to say a lady's pretty. But the whole point is, sir, that we can arrange things so that you and Miss Wilton don't always have to spend all your time looking after us kids. If you agree not to overdo the whacking and all that kind of school masterly thing, us older boys can make sure the rest don't get too out of hand. You and Miss Wilton lead your lives, we lead ours. Take it from me, sir, it really does work.'

Ben, of course, thought the whole thing sounded preposterous, but he had never been a prep school master before, and he had certainly never come across an institution like Portland Court. He looked down on the boy's open, smiling face and felt strangely reassured. He didn't understand why, but it suddenly struck him that, so long as Taylor was around, his life at the school would be quite bearable.

But he still couldn't forget that feeling of being watched when he had arrived. Who had that been? And what should he make of Hempson's warning about Taylor, followed so rapidly by Mr Spencer's warning about Hempson? He would have to be very careful, he was sure of that.

Chapter 2

Foster the Bully

'Lloyd George knew my fa-a-ther; Father knew Lloyd George.'

Taylor made out the words being sung to the familiar tune of Onward Christian Soldiers as he approached the classroom. He sighed as he pushed open the door. 'Come on, lads, cut it out. It's hardly Barker's fault.'

'Hey, how long have you been standing outside the door, Taylor?' Parsons had stopped his chanting as soon as Taylor came in.

'I haven't been. But it's pretty obvious what's going on.'

'You're spooky, Taylor.' Mitchell Major, just like the others, was taking time after the holidays to readjust to Taylor's uncanny ability to absorb the whole story from hearing just a few words. 'So, perhaps you'd like to tell us what's going on as you're so clever?'

Taylor grinned. 'Easy,' he said, 'my guess is that Barker got a bit miffed that the head asked me, not him, to show the new master round. He probably thought it was more a job for the head boy than for someone without any title at all. How am I doing?'

'Not bad,' Mitchell groaned as he realised that Taylor was right again. 'Go on.'

'Well, it all flows from that. One of you twits,' he grinned again as he used the word, 'probably said something about Barker only getting the title because his old man came up with the cash for the new bowling machine. Then you started singing Lloyd George at him, 'cos of buying honours. Anyway, like I said, it's not Barker's fault, and I bet he's going to be a terrific head boy.'

'Thanks, Taylor,' Barker gave his friend an affectionate punch on the shoulder, 'but they're right, of course. I mean, you'd be a much better head boy than I will be. And it's true I only got it 'cos my pater produced the lolly.'

'I don't agree,' Taylor was warming to his theme. 'Ok, maybe the money helped a bit, but you're absolutely cut out for it. I'd be hopeless. I'd have to stick to the rules and things like that. I'd never manage it.' He shuddered, 'I mean, think about it, can you really see me sending some poor kid to the head? I'm not saying you're a sneak or anything like that, Barker, but you're a lot more law abiding than I can ever be.'

He turned to the others. 'So, how about dropping all this Barker baiting? Who wants to know about the new beak?'

The six boys moved closer to him, all nodding eagerly, and in some trepidation.

Taylor paused, and then smiled a broad and immensely reassuring smile. 'He's going to be ok. He's a bit wet behind the ears, but he's probably only eighteen after all. The great thing is he fell for Miss Wilton the second he saw her, and she for him. So long as we keep the youngsters quiet most of the time he's not going to want to waste his energy on bossing kids around when he could be making eyes at our gorgeous under matron.'

There was an audible and united sigh of relief as his listeners realised that the disaster of the previous year was not to be repeated.

* * *

Mr Green, whom Taylor had prevailed upon to help, had one end of the trunk and Ben had the other. They were carrying it up the stairs to Ben's room.

'That boy Taylor seems rather a confident young chap. Is he head boy or just a prefect?'

'Neither,' said Mr Green, grimacing at the unaccustomed hard labour. 'For some reason I've never fathomed, we don't have any prefects, just a head boy. He's called Barker.'

'And is Barker as capable as Taylor?'

Mr Green chuckled. 'Goodness me, no. But he's got a frightfully rich father.'

'You mean he got the job just because of his father's money?' Ben was still young enough to be shocked by such things.

'What's wrong with that? Our meagre salaries have to be paid by someone, you know. Spencer daren't put up the fees to match other prep schools. There'd be a mass exodus of boys.'

'But isn't it rather hard on the other boys if the head boy's job can just be bought? Taylor struck me as being awfully bright, if a little cheeky. Shouldn't he have the chance to go for the job?'

'Oh, I shouldn't worry about Taylor,' Mr Green stopped on the landing and put the trunk down as he rubbed his lower back, 'he's quite content running the school, he doesn't need some grand title.'

'Running the school? What can you mean?'

'You'll see, dear boy,' he chuckled again, 'you'll see.' With a sigh he bent down to pick the trunk up again and they resumed their journey.

As they did so, Ben suddenly had, again, the feeling that someone was watching them.

* * *

'Right,' Taylor was getting back to business, 'any sign of new bug trouble from Foster?'

'Nothing yet,' said Mitchell Major, 'but I did see him whispering to a couple of his pals outside the first form. As soon as they saw me, they turned tail and went back into Shell.'

'He's a complete menace,' said Taylor with a sigh. 'Ok, I'd better have a word with the new bugs. I'd ask you to come along, Barker, but it might not be right for you to hear what I'll be saying.'

Barker grinned his understanding. 'Yes, I can imagine.'

Taylor left the classroom and made his way past Shell's room towards the first form. He'd seen the five new boys at tea but not yet been able to speak to them. Even so, his preliminary assessment had convinced him that one of them at least was probably going to need some extra help in coping with his new life as a boarder at Portland Court. And, knowing what he did about Foster, he guessed that it would be that one who became the bully's first target.

It was immediately noticeable that the sound coming from the first form's room was a great deal more subdued than that coming from the others. Taylor opened the door and walked in.

Yes, sure enough, one of the boys, the one he had identified earlier, was sitting apart from the other four. His face was expressionless, but Taylor guessed he was inwardly fighting to stop his terror being manifested to others. He wasn't by any means the smallest of the new crop. Neither did he display any other obvious sign of being a weed. His physique, if such things can be judged in an eight year old boy, looked to be that of a budding sportsman. He wasn't wearing glasses. But Taylor remained sure that the lad was suffering from a severe case of homesickness and, if he had detected that, a serial bully like Foster would spot it in an instant.

The four boys sitting together looked up as soon as the door opened. The fifth reacted more slowly, but did also look, a second or two later, to see who had come in.

Taylor smiled at them. 'Just popped in to welcome you to Portland. I'm Taylor. I'm in the sixth form.'

The news that this big boy was in the very top class in the school seemed to render the new boys dumb but, after a moment's thought, they scrambled to their feet in a show of the kind of respect they considered appropriate.

'No need for that,' Taylor waved them down again, 'I'm not head boy or anything. I'm just a normal boy like you lot. So, any of you got names? What about you?' He addressed this to the lone boy.

'Um,' he stammered, 'I'm, um I'm John ... I mean I'm Roberts.'

Taylor turned to the others who, one by one, gave their names without making Roberts's mistake.

'Good to meet you all.' He made his way to a chair next to Roberts's and sat down. 'So, Roberts, you got any brothers or sisters?'

'I've got a brother,' the boy's voice sounded strained and rather shaky, 'but he's only six.'

'That means you're used to being the boss. That's good. Will your bro be coming here when he's eight?'

Blushing slightly at the strange suggestion that he might be a boss, Roberts nodded.

'He's a lucky lad, then. He'll have an older bro here to keep an eye on him.'

Patiently, Taylor carried on with his apparently inconsequential small talk with Roberts, then, as the boy's contributions started to become more confident - sometimes even made with a hint of a smile - Taylor began to draw in the other boys. He knew it would be a mistake to rush into the important subject, but the time came when he thought it safe to get down to business.

'Right, lads, we've got some planning to do. This is one of the nicest schools in the land, but it does have the odd problem. Our problem this term is a boy in Shell called Foster. He's a decent chap most of the time, but he's got this thing about needing to show off to new bugs – that's you lot. I'm pretty sure he's going to try something after lights out tonight, and you've got to be ready for it. First thing, you need a leader. The trouble is you don't yet know each other, so there's not much point you trying to choose one. I'll do it for you.'

He paused, looking from one eager face to the next, apparently thinking hard and long about the choice. Finally he gave his decision. 'All five of you seem top rate lads, so it's not an easy choice, but I reckon it'll have to be Roberts.' He smiled at the others, 'You can tell me tomorrow if I got it wrong, but I don't think I have. Now,' he leant closer to his audience and they craned forward towards him, 'this is what you must do.'

* * *

Roberts had been half looking forward to bed time and half dreading it. Until Taylor's surprising announcement, he had chiefly been thinking that curling up under his bed clothes, shutting off the sounds of other boys and thinking of home would be almost a pleasure, though he was bright enough to realise that it was likely to be a pleasure mingled with tears. Now things were different. Some sort of raid could be expected at almost any time after lights out, or at least after lights out in Middle Dorm (where the Shell boys slept).

And the targets of the raid would be the five new boys. Taylor had been certain of that. Foster, and whichever other boys he managed to rope in, would not touch the five second form boys who also occupied Junior Dorm. In return, Taylor had explained, the second form boys would remain entirely neutral. That meant the new boys would be on their own, and their leader would be none other than Roberts himself.

As the five boys changed into their pyjamas, washed their hands and faces – it would be another five days before the first of their weekly baths – and brushed their teeth, all were thinking only of the raid. And what a burden of responsibility lay on Roberts's young shoulders. He could not, must not, let his new friends down. Above all he must not allow himself the luxury of letting his thoughts turn to home. He must be strong. He would be strong.

The really pretty under-matron, Miss Wilton, read them a story before lights out. It was from a Biggles book. Roberts liked Biggles, but he couldn't concentrate tonight. There was far too much racing through his head. At last she closed the book, smiled at the ten boys and left the dorm.

* * *

Ben was on his way to middle dorm to do lights out duty. He smiled rather nervously at Sarah as she came out of junior dorm. Would there be any chance of talking to her later? After all, the boys were asleep and all the other staff had gone off to the village, to the pub, if Taylor was right about these things. How miserable it would be if he and Sarah had to retire to their respective bedrooms. But he mustn't be too forward. He knew that.

'Hello,' she sounded so confident and bright, 'are you off to shut down middle dorm?'

What a wonderful smile she had. And had there ever been a girl with such perfect blonde hair, such shining blue eyes, such slim, long legs?

He coughed in embarrassment. 'Um, yes, I suppose so.'

Why did he have to be so gauche? Why couldn't he seem so at ease as she was? Maybe her smile meant she was laughing at him.

'I was wondering. What with everyone else being in the village, I don't see why we shouldn't use the masters' common room.'

Did she mean it? Was she really saying that they should be together, in the masters' common room, all evening?

'Well, Taylor did say something to me about the duty master and under matron using it in the evenings.'

Really. Why had he used Taylor? She must think him pathetic.

But she smiled again. 'Taylor does seem to be rather important. I'm sure if he says we can use it, it must be all right. I'll go down there now.'

* * *

Ben wondered if the boys of middle dorm noticed that he was blushing, and grinning rather inanely as he opened the door. Not that he minded if they did notice.

He stood in the doorway looking around. Most of the boys were in bed. But three of them seemed to be conducting a battle with towels, flicking each other and squealing with delight whenever they scored a hit. As soon as they saw him, they froze but, perhaps reassured by his grinning, they then resumed.

He forgot for a moment his assignation with Sarah. How should he react to this display? Should he be cross? Should he threaten dire punishment?

'What a pathetic lot you are.' The voice came from just behind him.

He turned and saw Taylor and, when he looked back, he saw the three boys suddenly rushing for their beds.

'Oh, hello, Taylor. You took the words out of my mouth.'

Ben suspected he sounded rather lame, but neither Taylor nor the middle dorm boys gave any indication that they thought so.

'Looks like you were lucky I came in when I did,' said Taylor, glaring at the offenders. 'Goodness knows what Mr Glossop would have done if I hadn't.'

As Ben studied the faces of the boys it struck him that it wasn't what he would have done that was on their minds.

* * *

Sarah was sitting at the end of the sofa. Would it be too forward to sit next to her? Ben looked around the room as he tried to make up his mind. Perhaps, tonight, the first night, it would be more seemly to sit on one of the armchairs. He started walking towards one.

'Why not sit here?' she was patting the cushion beside her.

'Oh, um, yes, jolly good.' "Jolly" again - what on earth was happening to him?

He changed direction and lowered himself onto the sofa, being careful to leave a good foot between them.

They sat in silence for a few seconds. Then, as tends to happen in such circumstances, both started to talk at the same time.

'No, it wasn't anything interesting,' Ben blushed again.

Sarah continued, 'I was just thinking about Roberts. He's one of the new boys.'

'That's extraordinary,' more blushing as he realised that his claim, true though it was, to have been about to raise the same topic might again be seen as too forward, as though he were claiming to be able to read her mind. 'I mean, well, I was thinking about him too. I was watching him at tea. He looked a picture of misery.'

'Exactly, but he was totally different at bed time. I'd always understood that the first night at boarding school was meant to be the worst for the type who gets homesick. But he didn't seem to be upset at all. I think,' she paused as she tried to find the right words, 'yes, that was it, I think he was preoccupied by something, but it wasn't something that distressed him.'

'How very strange.' Ben would have liked to come up with some startling insight to explain the boy's transformation, but it was beyond him. 'I wonder what was going through his mind.'

* * *

'When do you think they'll come?' Jameson, one of the new boys, was whispering. Talking after lights out, he guessed, was a pretty serious offence.

'I don't know,' Roberts's voice was even quieter. 'Taylor did say it would be silly of them to do it before senior dorm lights out, but I suppose we ought to get ready, just in case.' He got out of bed and tiptoed to the door, putting his ear to it as he checked that no master was around. 'Sounds like the coast's clear. Ok, let's take up our positions.'

* * *

All but one of the senior dorm boys were still in the boys' common room. Taylor was upstairs sitting on the edge of his bed, hoping Foster would not be so stupid as to launch his attack at a time when Ben or Sarah might be around. If either of them intervened before Roberts and his new friends could carry out their plan, the result might well be disastrous. He had even toyed with the idea of dropping a hint to Foster that he should wait until well past senior dorm lights out. But he had not done so. Any suggestion that he knew about the proposed raid would almost certainly lead to its postponement. That, Taylor was sure, would be a major lost opportunity.

* * *

‘Right you are, lads,’ Foster was climbing out of bed, his pillow in his right hand, ‘no time like the present. Let’s get going.’

‘Shouldn’t we wait till after senior dorm lights out?’ Baker was not convinced of the wisdom of the plan at all, but to carry it out just when that new master might be coming upstairs struck him as being folly on a grand scale.

‘Are you scared?’ There was a detectable sneer in Foster’s tone. ‘You don’t have to come, you know. Four of us will be easily enough to see off five new bugs.’

‘Of course I’m not scared.’ Why, Baker thought to himself, could he not be brave enough to stand up to such stupidity? Reluctantly, he pushed the bed clothes back, seized his pillow and got out of bed.

‘Good. Just remember, Roberts is mine. You lot can take who you want. I get Roberts.’

Baker had a feeling that Foster should have said “whom” not “who”, but he wasn’t sure. Anyway, this didn’t seem like the right moment to debate grammar.

* * *

Oh no. Taylor leant forward, listening intently. *Yes. There was movement in middle dorm. What idiots.*

He jumped up, tiptoed out onto the landing and found a spot in the shadows, near the top of the stairs. He would stand guard. He didn't know what he would be able to do, but he must be ready to do something.

* * *

Ben looked at his watch. He didn't want to leave the room, to leave Sarah, but he must not forget his duties.

'Senior dorm lights out in ten minutes,' he said. 'I thought I might pop up a bit early, give me a chance to have a chat with the boys, you know, get to know them a bit.'

'Good idea,' that wonderful smile again, 'they seem like a nice crowd, even if Taylor's a bit scary.' She laughed, taking any sting there might have been out of her description of the boy.

'I know what you mean. Do you know, Green said a funny thing to me earlier. He said Taylor runs the school. It's all a bit odd.'

He stood and made his way to the door.

* * *

Taylor's gaze was fixed on middle dorm's door. He was still praying that the noise he had heard did not signify the start of the raid, but his prayers weren't answered. The door slowly opened. Foster was leading. There were four other boys behind him. All had pillows in their hands. All looked terrifyingly large compared to their intended victims. 'Please,' Taylor almost spoke out loud, 'please let it work.'

He turned and looked over the railings, down towards the masters' common room. There was no sign of movement there. He turned back and watched the invaders creeping silently into junior dorm.

He held his breath.

* * *

'Wait for my order.' Foster's whisper sounded more like a hiss.

Each Shell boy made his way to a new boy's bed. Foster headed straight for Roberts. He grinned. It was an evil grin, one which, had it been light enough to see it, would have been enough on its own to show that he was up to no good.

He looked down on the sleeping body, completely covered by bed clothes. 'Probably blubbing,' he thought to himself.

He held the pillow in both hands. He raised it above his head. He glanced round and, with the help of the moonlight, saw that all the others were equally poised.

He opened his mouth to give the order.

'Now.'

But the voice was not his. It seemed to come from somewhere near the floor. He hesitated for a second. It was a second too long.

Suddenly, he felt a sharp pain in his right shin. Instinctively, he dropped the pillow and bent down to feel the injury.

That was all Roberts needed. In one bound he was out from under his bed and had grabbed Foster's pillow - his own was pretending to be a sleeping boy in the bed. A moment later he was standing above the bending ten year old, pillow raised high, and brought it down with all the force he could muster.

Foster crashed to the floor. Roberts glanced round. The same scene was being repeated by the other four beds.

It was working.

* * *

Taylor grimaced as he heard the noise from within junior dorm. He turned and looked again, down to the ground floor. As he did so, the masters' common room door opened.

The worst had happened. He felt sure that the pillow fight would at any moment spill out onto the landing, just as Ben got to the stairs.

He looked down. Ben's pace had increased. He had obviously heard. He was taking the stairs two at a time.

Taylor turned back to see the junior dorm door opening again. It was a minor consolation to see the four older boys, minus their pillows, scrambling to safety as the new boys pursued them.

He had to act.

He headed for Ben.

They met halfway, on the stairs.

'What on earth's going on?' Ben stopped for a second to interrogate Taylor.

'Oh, nothing to worry about, sir.' Taylor placed himself squarely in front of the master. 'It'll sort itself out. Just a first night tradition. I'll explain it in the morning.'

'No one told me about any first night tradition. Come on, out of my way, boy. I must investigate.'

'No, you mustn't, sir.' Had he gone too far? Probably, but he must press on. Out of the corner of his eye he saw Sarah emerging from the masters' common room. 'Hello, Ma'am, I hope you're settling in all right.'

Ben turned and looked down the stairs.

'What's up?' Sarah sounded much more composed than Ben had.

'There's some sort of fight going on. Taylor here is trying to stop me going up to deal with it.'

What could he say? He would have to risk something hinting at the truth.

'It's fine, Ma'am. It'll be over in a second. And ...' - would she understand? - 'Roberts will be the hero.'

'What nonsense are you talking, Taylor?' Now Ben sounded seriously cross.

But Sarah was smiling again. 'I won't pretend I've grasped it all,' she said as she climbed the stairs, 'but well done, Taylor.'

He let out a long sigh of relief. She had got it.

'Would I be right,' she had now reached them, 'in thinking it might not be politic for you to tell us precisely what is going on upstairs?'

Taylor was at last grinning. 'It could be better if we just left things as they are.'

'I thought so. Come on, let's all go downstairs for five minutes. You can show us where everything's kept in the masters' common room. I'm sure you must know.'

Ben stared at the boy and the beautiful girl, and opened and shut his mouth a couple of times. Then he found his voice. 'Would someone please explain what is going on?' This time he sounded confused rather than angry.

'My guess,' Sarah tugged at his sleeve, 'is that Taylor has set Roberts some important task which, if carried through, will result in his becoming the hero of the first form. But I don't think we should pry too deeply. Come along, you can always check on the other dorms when you go up for the seniors lights out.'

Ben surrendered. With one last glance up the stairs he turned and walked down again.

* * *

The new boys had surrounded their attackers and pillows were raining down at an alarming rate on their defenceless heads.

At last Foster spoke. 'Ok, we give in. You've won. But you've got to stop before Mr Glossop hears. We'll all be for it then.'

Roberts's face lit up in delight. 'All right, but you'd better not try it again. Stop lads, head for the door. Leave their pillows there.'

* * *

Ben didn't have much of a chance for a chat with the boys of senior dorm before lights out. He still didn't quite understand what had happened, but his check on middle and junior dorms revealed nothing other than boys apparently sleeping in their beds. He couldn't see, of course, the almost manic grin on Roberts's face.

And then, as he went back down the stairs, there was the certainty, yet again, that he was being watched.

Chapter 3

Snowed In

The weather was extraordinary for November. Ben had rather doubted the wisdom of all his teaching colleagues piling into Mr Spencer's Morris Minor Traveller to make the perilous journey through snow drifts to the village pub. Not only was there an obvious risk they would not be able to reach their destination, but there was also the equally obvious risk, with the snow continuing to fall, that the return journey would prove impossible as well.

But the other masters had been adamant.

'A valuable lesson for the boys,' opined Mr Rice (Latin, Greek and the boiler). 'Shows them that we can stand up to the elements.'

'Excellent point,' said Mr Green (French, woodwork and vegetable gardener). 'It may be tough for us, but it's our duty to battle through.'

Ben had wondered, at the time whether this hardy group of prep school masters would also see it as their duty to battle their way out of the pub and back to the school, but he had said nothing.

Now he had his answer.

'Is that you, Glossop?' The voice was instantly recognisable as belonging to Mr Spencer, headmaster and proprietor of the school. 'Not a very good line.'

Ben could hear a buzz of conversation in the background, interspersed with hearty laughs.

'Yes, headmaster, Glossop speaking.'

'Bad news, I'm afraid.' He was shouting over the noise. 'Conditions have worsened. It would be foolhardy of us to attempt to get back tonight. The landlord here has decently offered us beds for the night, so you, Matron and Miss Wilton will have to look after things on your own.'

Ben managed to stifle the sigh. 'Very well, headmaster. Do you have any idea when you might make it back?'

'Can't say, old boy, but I think you're going to have to work on the assumption that you'll have to put all the boys in one classroom tomorrow.'

Ben was entirely used to coping with the boys without help from the other masters in the evenings. But actually teaching the whole school on his own was not something he had tried before. Sarah Wilton, angel that she was (this time he did sigh), would do all she could to help - he knew that - but Matron was very unlikely to lend a hand.

Miss Stafford, charmingly known as the 'elephant' by the boys, had already made her displeasure clear. She had been just as eager as the masters to make the trip to the pub and she had been predictably put out when Mr Spencer had explained they could only take one car and that it would be a tight enough fit with just the six masters. He could, perhaps, have phrased it more politely, without giving the impression that her magnificent size was an impediment.

Anyway, Matron had stormed off to her room armed with a bottle of gin purloined from the masters' common room, and Ben knew her well enough to realise that he would be unlikely to be seeing her again for quite a time.

* * *

The news spread to the boys at an alarming speed, and it was highly welcome news too.

'This is just the best thing that could happen.' Taylor, adopting his usual role of leader, was standing on a table in the boys' common room and addressing the ten other senior boys who had not yet gone to their dormitory. 'I heard the weather forecast on the Home Service and they said the snow's going to go on for days. Just think, lads, we might have weeks of school with only Gusset Twanger in charge.' "Gusset Twanger", it should be explained, had been chosen as Ben Glossop's nickname after some rather wild speculation in senior dorm about what he got up to with Miss Wilton when they were on their own together.

The boys eagerly fell to planning how they would advise Ben to occupy their time during the next day. They were absolutely agreed, (well, it was obvious, wasn't it?), that lessons would be quite out of the question. One master could never be expected to teach thirty boys at the same time. So other projects would have to be arranged.

Suggestions flew around the room until at last Taylor raised his commanding hand and made his pronouncement. 'It's got to be the Messerschmitt,' he declared, 'this is our best chance ever. With Himmler safely in the pub for days, we can really get it done.'

"Himmler" was Mr Hempson (Geography, English and drains). He was the newest of the older masters, having arrived at the school at the beginning of the previous academic year. He and Mr Staughton, Ben's predecessor as gap year teacher, had been firm allies, both of them, as Taylor would put it, seeming to think that "whacking" was the main job of a schoolmaster.

And there had been one offence in particular that had aroused their ire more than any other: any boy caught anywhere near the part of the woods in which legend had it that a German fighter plane was buried could be sure of regretting his actions.

Quite why the two masters were so exercised about the Messerschmitt was a mystery. True, that part of the woods had always been out of bounds, but no other master had ever suggested that breaking the rule was close to high treason. Now, Taylor and his friends reasoned, there would be a splendid opportunity to do some digging. After all, if they had Ben with them, there could be no danger. He would make sure there were no injuries (the presumed reason for the site being out of bounds).

But, vastly more importantly, "Himmler" would not be able to stop them.

* * *

'Oh, Ma'am.' Miss Wilton was wishing the boys in senior dorm a good night and Taylor was pleading with her. 'Please persuade him. It'll be such fun and frightfully educational as well. Just imagine, we might find the corpse of the German pilot; that would be so good for our science lessons.'

Sarah grimaced. 'What a gruesome thought, Taylor. I hardly think that that's going to be your best argument with Mr Glossop.'

'Maybe not,' he thought for a moment, 'but I bet we can learn simply masses about nature by working outside in all this snow. I mean, animal footprints and what happens to leaves and things when they get all iced up.'

Sarah smiled, 'I've never known you boys to be so keen on learning.' She paused. 'Well, maybe I'll have a word with Mr Glossop for you.'

'Oh, Ma'am, you're just the best,' screeched Parsons from across the room.

The boys had known that their only real hope lay in persuading Sarah. Ben, they were convinced, would do absolutely anything for the beautiful Under Matron. And they were right, of course.

* * *

'Don't you think Mr Spencer might think it a little irresponsible of us to spend the day playing in the snow with the boys?'

Ben was clearly not wholly opposed to Sarah's suggestion of an expedition into the woods, but he needed some reassurance.

'I'm not sure Mr Spencer is qualified to form a judgment on responsible behaviour,' Sarah pressed her point home. 'I don't see how a headmaster who takes almost all the teaching staff off to a pub in a blizzard can possibly complain about the one remaining master deciding to take the boys on a nature trail.'

As she spoke the telephone rang.

Ben picked up the receiver. 'Glossop, is that you?' It was Mr Spencer again.

'Yes, headmaster.'

'All well?'

'Yes. The boys are in bed. Miss Wilton and I were just discussing our plans for tomorrow.'

'Jolly good. I'm afraid there'll be no chance of our getting back for a day or two, but I'm sure you'll cope splendidly. The thing to do, my boy, is to make use of this weather. Don't even try formal teaching. Quite impossible in the circumstances. Take the boys out into the snow.'

Ben smiled at Sarah. 'An excellent idea, headmaster. Funnily enough, we were just wondering whether there might not be something to be said for going in search of the German 'plane the boys keep talking about.'

'What a brilliant plan. Yes, that's exactly what you must do. An archaeological expedition. Very educational.'

Ben gave Sarah a wink. 'That's what we thought, headmaster, and the boys can write an essay about it afterwards.'

'You're a born schoolmaster, Glossop. Well done. Can't stay

chatting, much as I'd love to. Got to get back to our curriculum meeting. No rest for the wicked.'

Ben may not have been at Portland Court for long, but he had a pretty good idea of what form a "curriculum meeting" in the village pub would probably take.

* * *

'Good work, Green.' The headmaster was relieved to see that Mr Green had managed, by handing over an IOU note, to acquire another round of drinks. 'I've just been speaking to Glossop. He's coping with the crisis magnificently. I grant you, he has the easier task. but that's as it should be. Better by far that we should be the ones facing the real ordeal.'

'True, headmaster,' Mr Rice managed to control his hiccoughs for a moment, 'I would be feeling enormously guilty if I were safely back at Portland Court while the rest of you were stuck in the village. Does Glossop have a plan for tomorrow?'

'Indeed he has and a splendid one it is too. He's going to take the boys into the woods and try to find that German 'plane.'

There was a sudden spluttering from across the table. Mr Spencer looked up and saw beer dribbling down Mr Hempson's chin.

‘Gone down the wrong way, Hempson?’

Mr Hempson wiped the liquid from his face with his sleeve. ‘What did you say, headmaster?’

‘I asked whether your beer had gone down the wrong way.’

‘No; before that. What is it Glossop’s going to do?’

If Mr Spencer noticed his younger colleague’s ashen complexion he gave no sign of having done so. ‘He’s going to take them into the woods to find the Messerschmitt.’

‘But that’s appalling.’ Mr Hempson jumped up from his seat. ‘We must telephone and stop him.’

Mr Spencer and the other masters were genuinely perplexed.

‘Why should we stop him?’ Mr Green asked.

‘Well, it’s obvious. I mean, well, we all know. That bit of the woods is out of bounds. We can’t let the boys go there. No, we must stop this mad plan.’ He tried to push his way past Mr Rice to get to the public telephone.

Mr Rice did not clear a path. ‘Don’t talk rot, man,’ he said. ‘Glossop is quite capable of looking after the boys’ safety.’

‘But, don’t you see,’ Mr Hempson looked round at the other masters, ‘once the boys have been allowed to go there with a master, they’ll think it’s perfectly all right to go there on their own? No, it has to be stopped.’

He pushed roughly past Mr Rice and headed for the telephone, only to be intercepted by the landlord.

'Sorry, sir, if it's the telephone you're after, I'm afraid the line's down.'

Mr Hempson glared at the publican. 'What on earth do you mean?' he shouted. 'This is an emergency. I have to speak to Portland Court.'

'That may be the case, sir, but it can't be done.'

'Nonsense, of course it can be done. You must get the line up again.'

'And how do you propose I do that, sir?'

Mr Hempson looked back at his colleagues. 'We have to do something. Surely you see that?' He turned to face the door. 'If this pub can't keep its telephone line open,' now he sounded petulant, 'we must get back to the school as quickly as possible.' He strode towards the door.

'Hempson!' Mr Spencer had many years' experience of shouting surnames in a threatening manner. True, he had not often had to use that particular talent on masters, but things were now getting out of hand. The landlord's patience was being tested: the currency of IOU notes might not be accepted for much longer. 'Sit down at once!'

Mr Hempson had almost reached the door as he heard the barked command. There was something in the tone that seemed to get through to him.

He stopped and turned to his employer. 'But, headmaster, we just can't let this happen.' He was pleading. 'This could be such a disaster for the school.'

'There is nothing, nothing at all, we can do,' Mr Spencer's voice was quieter but it was still the voice of a headmaster in his prime. 'I have no idea why you are so exercised by Glossop's plans, but since we have all agreed that he will able to prevent a "disaster" tomorrow, let us not worry about what may happen in days to come.'

It should have worked but Mr Hempson was plainly convinced action was required now.

'No, headmaster,' and he turned back to the door, 'I must go back to the school. It is my duty to protect the boys.'

Mr Rice stood and made as to go to stop Hempson.

Mr Spencer waved him down. 'Let him go. The man is obviously deranged, but he won't get far.'

Mr Hempson certainly didn't get far. The door opened outwards. He pushed at it with as much energy as he could muster, but there had obviously been a further heavy fall of snow. It wouldn't budge.

Not only were the telephone lines down, but there was no prospect of anyone getting out of the pub. After some minutes of trying, he reluctantly returned to the table.

He sat heavily in his chair, put his elbows on the table and rested his head in his hands. 'This is just dreadful. We have to find a way to stop it.'

For the next hour the other masters did their best to ignore Mr Hempson's groans of distress and they made no complaint when he announced that he would go to bed in the hope that conditions would have improved enough to enable him to get back to the school in the early morning.

He had a restless night. If anything, he looked even whiter when he rose in the morning than he had looked when he'd gone to bed. And, when he found the front door of the pub as immovable as it had been the night before, he seemed to be in the deepest despair.

* * *

So it was, after a less fraught breakfast at Portland Court, that Ben and Sarah found themselves leading a line of excited boys across the snow-laden fields to the woods.

There was no doubt that the school grounds looked magical in these conditions. The snow masked the badly neglected lawns and the silvery rime on the trees made them look as though they had come straight out of a fairy tale. While they were still some way off from their destination, a large crow suddenly flew out of the trees and dived down towards the field. The contrast of its blackness against the white of the snow was almost breathtaking.

As they got to the edge of the woods, Ben held his hand up to stop them. 'Now,' he said, 'who reckons he knows which bit we're aiming for?'

'I do, sir.' Predictably, it was Taylor who spoke. 'Vesuv .... I mean Mr Staughton, sir, caught me trying to find it last year. I could tell I was close because he got really angry when he saw where I was. I mean really, truly angry, sir - six of the best angry, if you know what I mean.'

Taylor was invited to lead the way. The thirty boys, Ben and Sarah wrestled their way through the undergrowth. After he had got about a hundred yards into the wood, Taylor suddenly stopped, holding his hand high to indicate to the others that they, too, should stop.

'What is it, Taylor?' asked Ben.

'Quiet, sir,' hissed the boy in a manner which many school masters may well have thought to be a little disrespectful. Then, signalling to the others to stay where they were, he crept forward, peering intently ahead.

Such was Taylor's natural quality of leadership that neither the other boys nor the master and Under Matron even considered disobeying his instruction. After a few minutes he crept back and leant up to whisper into Ben's ear.

'It's Vesuvius, sir, Mr Staughton. I mean, he's digging where the Messerschmitt is, sir.'

'Is this a joke, Taylor?' Ben asked, in a whisper that showed he doubted very much whether it was a joke. 'Mr Staughton left the school in his second term. He can't possibly be here now.'

'But he is, sir,' insisted the boy, 'and he shouldn't be. It's private property, sir. It belongs to Mr Spencer.'

Ben thought for a second.

'Very well, Taylor,' he was still whispering, 'show me.' He turned to the others, signalling them to stay where they were, and followed his twelve year old guide.

Sure enough, as they inched their way between the trees, Ben could see the figure of a man, about his own age, furiously digging the hard ground with a large spade.

He stopped and whispered to Taylor, 'Taylor, do you swear to me, on pain of suffering a whacking ten times harder than Mr Staughton ever gave you, that that man is indeed Mr Staughton?'

Taylor looked up, his eyes shining with honesty. 'I promise, sir.'

They were now about twenty yards from the disgraced former junior master. Amazingly, though, they had not been spotted, so intent was "Vesuvius" on his task.

'Right,' said Ben, in a tone which revealed his own powers of leadership, 'this is what we'll do.'

Five minutes later, Ben, Sarah and the thirty boys had formed themselves into a wide circle around the still unaware Staughton. All watched closely. None made a sound, even the youngest eight year old was determined not to let the side down.

They waited.

Staughton dug and dug. The work must have been exhausting but something was driving him on. Never for a moment did he pause. Not once did he look up or around.

Then, at last, with a little shriek of delight, he threw the spade to the ground and jumped down into the hole he had created.

Ben, who had been crouching down, stood in anticipation of Staughton's next move. He didn't have to wait long.

With a bound, Staughton was out of the hole clutching a large wooden box to his chest.

It was at that moment that he saw a line of prep school boys facing him. He had not yet seen Ben or Sarah.

He staggered back, showing his guilt with every movement of his body. He turned, as though to run from the boys, but then saw yet more. He turned again and saw Ben and Sarah. He opened his mouth as though to speak but, as he did so, the bottom of the wooden box, which had clearly become rotten in the earth, fell to the ground, followed swiftly by several bundles of paper.

'Hey, sir,' yelled Parsons to Ben, 'I know what they are. They're counterfeit pound notes. The Germans used to drop them in the War. I know because my Pater's job was to identify them for the Bank of England. We've got some at home.'

Mr Staughton dropped the remainder of the box and charged hard towards the smallest boys he could see.

It was Taylor who was the hero of the hour. Remembering all too well what "Vesuvius" had done to him when he had thought of digging up the Messerschmitt, he was now determined that his former master should not escape.

He threw himself at the fleeing man with such force that Staughton fell to the hard, stony ground. In a second, a heap of small boys, many of them with their own excellent reasons for being unconcerned about injuring him, was on top of the struggling master.

He was done for. There was no escape.

* * *

One could almost feel sorry for Mr Staughton. He was dragged back to the school and locked in the boot room. There he stayed, occasionally being fed school food of the most indigestible kind, for the three days that it took for the roads to be cleared sufficiently to allow the police through.

By the time they arrived, he was far too worn down to make any attempt at denying what he had been doing. He readily admitted to conspiring with Mr Hempson - he said it was Mr Hempson's idea in the first place - to flood the county with forged one pound notes which they knew to have come down with the doomed Messerschmitt.

Mr Hempson, together with the other five masters who had been snowed into the village pub, was a little the worse for wear when the police caught up with him on his return to the school. Maybe they should have waited until he was sober before questioning him, but they didn't see the point. It took them half an hour to get a full confession out of him. Taylor and several other senior boys didn't disguise their delight when they saw “Himmler” being dragged to the waiting police van.

As it moved off down the drive, Taylor rushed to the school bell and tugged several times at the rope. Ben and Sarah, hearing the chimes at an hour when they would not be expected to be heard, came into the hall and saw the boy, still pulling the rope and grinning like a Cheshire cat.

'Taylor, what on earth are you doing?' asked Ben.

'Sir,' he paused his tugging to explain, 'I am sounding the death knell of hypocrisy in this school. Good has triumphed over evil. Mr Glossop and Miss Wilton have triumphed over Himmler and Vesuvius. The Bleak Midwinter has brought forth Spring.'

Ben smiled. This was a very odd school but any institution which could boast a boy like Taylor could never be written off entirely. He turned to Sarah and, looking into her sparkling blue eyes, resolved that, at least as long as she and Taylor were there, he would remain a master at Portland Court.

What did it matter that he was being spied on? He knew he was being watched. He had felt it again that very day, but, somehow, he felt safe while Taylor was about.

Chapter 4

Coping With a Crisis

'Mr Hempson's departure poses something of a problem for us.' Mr Spencer was addressing the masters over a glass of sherry in the masters' common room. That is to say, he was addressing all the masters other than Ben, who was supervising the boys. 'It is far too late in the term for us to have any hope of finding a replacement, so I am afraid we're all going to have to take on extra duties.'

His audience began to shift uneasily in their seats: all considered their existing workloads to be quite arduous enough. The thought of having to take on more teaching duties, or even to take on the maintenance of the school drains, was not a pleasant one.

'I will say at once,' Mr Spencer was now using his magnanimous tone, 'that I certainly do not intend shirking myself.' He paused and all wondered which of Mr Hempson's tasks he would volunteer to tackle. 'I confess that, at my age, I do not relish the idea of having to suppress pillow fights and unearth hidden supplies of tuck intended for midnight feasts, but I am prepared to set a good example to the rest of you. I will take Hempson's place on the duty master rota.'

A new master, unaccustomed to Mr Spencer's ways, may well have found it impossible to keep silent on hearing this preposterous statement. After all, the whole school knew the headmaster had successfully persuaded Ben Glossop to act as duty master every evening and night, thereby allowing the older members of staff go to the village pub for well-earned refreshment. But Mr Spencer was not addressing any new masters.

'I must say, headmaster,' said Mr Green, 'that is extraordinarily noble of you.'

'Indeed,' said Mr Rice, nodding furiously in agreement.

'If a headmaster can't get his own hands dirty, so to speak, at a time like this,' said Mr Spencer attempting a look of modesty, 'he has no right to hold the post. No, I shall not plead age and seniority in order to avoid this additional labour, and I trust I shall undertake the work without complaint. But I am afraid we are still left with finding people to take on English, Geography and drains. Does anyone have any suggestions?'

'This really is troublesome,' said Mr Rice, taking rather a large swig from his sherry glass. 'I don't mind telling you, headmaster, that I have thought long and hard about how I might be able to help the school in its hour of need, but it is far from easy. I would love to add the drains to my portfolio, so to speak, but the boiler is somewhat temperamental and I just can't see how I can risk spending time on the drains when the water heating may suffer.'

Mr Green knew exactly what was expected of him. He spoke without any hesitation. 'I was wondering, headmaster, whether it might not be appropriate to ask young Glossop whether he would mind assuming responsibility for the drains. After all, his only non-teaching duty at present is looking after the games pitches and all this snow has rather put that on the back burner.'

Again, a newcomer might have protested that it was a little unfair on Ben, whose working hours were already at least twice as long as anyone else's and whose pay was less than half of the lowest paid of his colleagues, to give him yet another job. But, if such a thought crossed the mind of anyone in the common room that evening, no one expressed it.

'A first class idea, Green,' said Mr Spencer, 'Glossop is our man. I'm sure he will be very grateful to have been considered for such an important job.'

'I would dearly love,' said Mr Green, basking in the head master's approval, 'to take on more teaching. But I have to think of next term's common entrance examinations. I can't let the boys down. I only have three free periods a day to plan our approach to the examinations. I would be failing the school if I gave any of them up now.'

Mr Pine, who tended not to contribute very much to these discussions, now cleared his throat and put forward a suggestion of his own.

'I was only thinking the other day,' he said, 'that there would be a lot to be said for making more use of the senior boys. It must be part of our role to prepare them for the responsibilities of life in the world. It occurs to me that this is an excellent opportunity for us to give one of the older boys a real chance to prove himself.' The history master, feeling embarrassed at having made such a long speech, decided it would be prudent to say no more.

Even Mr Spencer had not thought of using a boy for teaching, but his mind was always open to new ideas, especially to ones which might save money. 'Please, go on, Pine. Develop your idea.'

Mr Pine blushed as he realised he had become the centre of attention, but he knew, having embarked on his suggestion, that he had no choice but to continue.

'Well, what I was wondering was whether we might re-arrange the timetable. Glossop could take over Hempson's senior school English lessons and one of the boys - Taylor would be the obvious choice - could do Glossop's junior school English. I do understand,' he rushed on before anyone could protest, 'that Taylor would need a lot of guidance, but Glossop could give him that.' Again, he ground to a halt.

The room was silent for a moment, then, positively beaming, Mr Spencer gave his verdict.

'What an absolutely capital idea. Pine, you are a genius. And what a wonderful opportunity for Taylor. There can't be a public school in the land that wouldn't jump at a boy who had discharged such duties. Yes, Taylor shall be given his chance.' Mr Spencer paused again as he pondered on the possibility of using boys for teaching in the long, as well as the short, term. Maybe, what a charming thought, Mr Hempson would never have to be replaced at all. A whole salary could be saved.

But the problem of Geography remained.

'We do still need to cover the geography lessons,' Mr Spencer said. 'Does anyone have any notion about how we can do that?'

'For a moment or two,' said Mr Pine, 'I did think I might be able to offer my services there, but the timetable simply doesn't allow it.'

It was Mr Green who came up with the solution.

'I wonder if I might observe,' he said, 'that it would only take a very slight alteration to the timetable to permit young Glossop to take on Hempson's geography classes. I have no doubt at all that he would be deeply grateful to you, headmaster, if you were to offer him the chance to expand his teaching experience to include geography. It may be he will decide on some less noble profession than school mastering when he comes down from the university, but he would be foolish to reject an opportunity like this one.'

Mr Spencer jumped to his feet.

'Oh well done, Green,' he exclaimed, 'you are so right. What a lucky young man Glossop is. Splendid, all our problems resolved. I think, gentlemen, that we thoroughly deserve another glass of sherry. We have demonstrated true British spirit. Undaunted by what may have appeared to be insuperable difficulties, we have, by the exercise of intelligence and selflessness, conquered our foes.'

Mr Spencer would have been quite happy to continue in this vein for several more minutes, but Mr Rice was thoroughly experienced at stemming the headmaster's sub-Churchillian oratory. He bounded to the drinks table, grabbed the decanter and rushed to replenish his employer's glass.

It did the trick. Tempting though it was to expand on his theme, it was more tempting to raise the schooner to his lips. The danger had passed; all could now relax.

Except that Matron chose that moment to come in.

'Ah, Matron, how nice to see you,' said Mr Spencer. 'I do hope you are now feeling better.'

'Only slightly,' said Matron, who had still not forgotten her distress at being left at the school when everyone else (except Ben and Sarah) had gone to the village pub and been snowed in. 'All this trouble over Mr Hempson has been a dreadful shock. I wonder if there might be a drop of gin here? I'm not a drinker normally, but I do think a small tincture might calm my nerves.'

'Of course, Matron,' Mr Spencer walked towards the drinks table, 'a bottle went missing the night of the great snow fall, but there's another here.'

'Oh, how awful, headmaster,' Matron managed to sound genuinely shocked. 'I suppose it must have been Hempson's accomplice.'

'I dare say, Matron,' the headmaster winked at Mr Green as he passed him. 'I really ought to have thanked you, by the way, for looking after the school while we were stranded in the village. I do hope it wasn't too awful for you.'

'I won't pretend,' replied Matron, who had spent the whole time in her room with the missing bottle of gin, 'that it was easy. Young Glossop and the Wilton girl have hearts of gold, but they're not of an age to be able to cope with that sort of crisis on their own. I just pray that all my labours over that awful period haven't completely exhausted me.' She paused while she swallowed a surprisingly large quantity of pink gin. 'Indeed, I was wondering, headmaster, whether it might not be prudent for some of my more mundane duties to be handed over to the Wilton girl? I ask only because I have the best interests of the school at heart. I couldn't bear to collapse from over-work and then blame myself for the chaos that would be bound to follow from my indisposition.' She smiled sweetly (or as sweetly as she could manage) and took another long draught of gin.

Mr Spencer thought for a moment before concluding it might not be wise to upset Matron further.

'Of course, Matron, we must do all we can to keep you fit and healthy. I have no doubt Miss Wilton will understand. She shall take over your night duties until you have recovered from our recent trials.'

No one was so insensitive as to point out that the removal of her night duties left only an hour or so of work every morning for Matron. Instead, Mr Green busied himself with the sherry decanter (and the gin for Matron) and proposed a toast.

'Matron and gentlemen, please raise your glasses. It would, I believe, be false modesty of the worst kind not to acknowledge what we have all done this evening to keep this great school afloat. Every one of us has put the school first and our own interests last. It is fitting, I think, to drink to "the senior staff of Portland".'

All raised their glasses and echoed Mr Green's words.

The crisis was over.

Chapter 5

The New Pupil

Taylor's appointment as a part-time school master at the advanced age of 12 was not the only interesting news Ben had to impart.

'Now, Taylor, before you go,' said the young master, 'there's something else I want you to do.'

'Of course, sir,' said Taylor, wondering what other important job the masters had dreamt up for him, 'just tell me what it is and I'll get on with it.'

'We have a new pupil arriving tomorrow.'

'A bit of an odd time for a new boy to arrive isn't it, sir? I mean, we're nearly half way through the term.'

'Yes. I'm not sure of the full story, but I gather the child is being moved from another boarding school so as to be closer to home. The father, he's a widower, lives in the village.'

'So does that mean he'll be a day boy?'

'No, the father has to work abroad a lot, so he wants to stick to boarding for his children.'

'It'll be a bit odd boarding just a mile from your home, I should think. How old is he?'

'Twelve, your age. That's why I wanted you to make sure she settles in.'

Taylor didn't immediately register the import of Ben's words. He started to respond, saying he would, of course, take on that responsibility. But, as he opened his mouth to speak, he suddenly realised what Ben had said. For a second or two his mouth opened and shut, like a fish's, then he managed to find words.

'Sir, did I hear you right. Did you say "she"?'

'I did. Yes, Portland Court is to have its first girl pupil. Should be rather interesting, don't you think?'

Taylor thought it would be absolutely appalling. His mind raced with thoughts of the havoc a girl could cause to his comfortable schoolboy life.

'But, sir,' his shock was enough to make him stammer, 'I mean, but, well, it's, well, it's ...'

'Spit it out, boy,' said Ben, smiling at the confusion he had caused to the usually self-confident pupil.

'Well, what I mean, sir,' he took a deep breath to regain his composure, 'is that you can't have girls in a boys' school.'

'Why not? There are plenty of co-educational schools around.'

'Yes, sir, but they've been sort of designed for girls as well as boys. You know, they have things like games mistresses to take the girls for Lacrosse and things like that, while masters take the boys for rugger and football. You're not going to make us boys play sissy games are you, sir? And I bet the boys in those schools don't have to share their common room with the girls. Anyway, where's she going to sleep? And,' he was now in full flow, 'she won't have any friends to play with. She'll have a rotten time, sir.'

Ben was still smiling. 'Let me see if I can deal with each of those concerns in turn. As to games, there will be no changes at all. I understand she is rather keen to play a bit of football.'

Taylor almost turned white with shock. He couldn't help interrupting.

'Oh no, sir, we can't let a girl play football with us. What would other schools say if they found out?'

'Don't worry. I dare say she won't be good enough to make a team. Where was I? Oh yes, sleeping arrangements. She will have a room on the top floor, the empty one next to Miss Wilton's.'

'Gosh, lucky thing,' Taylor blushed, 'I mean having a room on her own, sir, not being next to Miss Wilton.' Realising he sounded rude, he continued, 'I mean, Miss Wilton is one of the best, sir.' He could tell that his face must now be scarlet. 'Anyway, it'll be nice for the girl to have that room.'

'As for friends, of course she'll have them. You, to start with, are going to be an excellent friend to her.'

'Well,' Taylor was pleased to have got off the subject of the joys of being in a room next to the beautiful Under Matron's, 'I'll obviously do my best, sir, but it's not going to be easy. I don't really know how to talk about dolls and dancing and things like that. But I'll try.'

'I knew I could rely on you. She'll be arriving after church tomorrow. As soon as you get back, come to the main entrance. I'll be there as well, so there's no need to be too frightened. Her name, by the way, is Samantha Watson.'

'Right, sir, but what do we call her? I don't suppose you can call girls by their surnames. But Samantha's a bit of a sissy name. Maybe she'll agree to be "Sam" while she's here.'

'We'll find out tomorrow. Off you go now and give the others the good news.'

It was Saturday evening - no lessons, no prep. The other boys, Taylor knew, would be in the common room. As he walked to join them, his feelings were mixed. On the one hand, being the bearer of such astounding news was not something to be missed. On the other, there was the tricky matter of his own role in looking after Samantha. That, he was certain, would lead to endless ribbing. Still, he knew how to deal with that sort of thing.

The reaction in the common room was entirely predictable. All of them were horrified by Taylor's news. All were sure the pleasant lifestyle to which they were used would now be ruined.

Parsons summed it up. 'What if she annoys us? You can't fight with a girl. And I bet she'll be an awful sneak. My sister is and she's a girl.'

Once the immediate shock had worn off, the teasing of Taylor began, but he was ready for it. He only had to knock two boys to the ground before the others got the message. It was useful being the best fighter in the school.

* * *

The next morning the crocodile of boys made its way back from the village church to the school. Taylor was right at the back and was embarrassed to find he was feeling quite nervous as the moment of his meeting with Samantha approached. There were as many butterflies in his tummy as there were when he was standing outside Mr Spencer's study. He tried, as he did on those disagreeable occasions, to think of the next school match, but it didn't work - it never did. His mind kept returning to what lay in store for him in a few minutes' time.

He peeled off when they got to the main entrance. The other boys continued on their way to the side entrance, several of them looking back to Taylor and making faces which, were there not masters about, would have resulted in some fairly nasty bruising.

Ben and Sarah were standing outside the porch waiting for the great arrival. Both could tell that Taylor was less than his usual confident self. They smiled at him but thought it better not to burden him with small talk.

Fortunately, they didn't have to wait long. A few minutes later, a large Bentley purred up the drive. It was the sort of car, Taylor thought, that ought to have a chauffeur, but the man at the wheel was obviously not a chauffeur. He was about thirty-five, strikingly handsome and wearing a polo neck jersey. Beside him sat the girl, Samantha.

The man got out first. He was tall - over six feet. He had the bearing of someone who was used to getting his own way but there was also something about his eyes which convinced Taylor that he was a naturally kind man. He approached Ben, hand outstretched.

As her father was greeting Ben and Sarah, Samantha got out of the car and Taylor got his first proper look at her. Several things struck him at once.

She was wearing exactly the same uniform - grey shorts, white shirt and purple blazer - as the boys wore. That, Taylor thought, was a good sign. Although her face was definitely pretty, it didn't have a sissy look to it, and her hair, though longer than his, was not that long. There was certainly no horrid pony tail or bob. The really surprising thing, to Taylor, was to see that she was about his own height (and he was the tallest boy in the school). He had assumed, without consciously thinking about it, that she would be a lot smaller, being a girl, but she wasn't. For some reason which Taylor couldn't fathom, he found it strangely difficult not to stare at her long slim legs.

She clearly shared her father's self-confidence. She was walking towards Taylor, smiling (rather charmingly he thought) with her hand out.

'Hello,' she said, and, much to Taylor's consternation, he found himself thinking what a lovely voice she had, 'I'm Sam Watson.'

He took her hand in his and felt an odd shivery sensation run through his body. For a second he wondered if he was ill. He just couldn't understand why he was having all these strange feelings. Then he remembered his manners.

'I'm Taylor,' he said. 'I'm to show you round and things like that.'

'Sorry about saying my first name,' she was still smiling, 'I suppose I should have said "I'm Watson". I'll try to remember in future.'

'Oh, gosh, that doesn't matter. Anyway, being a girl we'll have to call you by your first name.'

The smile left her lips for a second. 'I certainly hope you don't,' she said, 'I don't want to be treated any differently from the rest of you.'

Ben interrupted them and introduced Taylor to Sam's father.

'This is the boy who'll be helping Sam settle in. I wouldn't say he was an angel, but he's thoroughly reliable.'

Mr Watson smiled down at Taylor. 'Well, you'd get pretty short shrift from Sam if you were an angel. Best of luck trying to keep her under control - you'll need it.'

* * *

It was agreed that Taylor and Sam, or Watson as we must now think of her, would go on a tour of the school and come back to say their goodbyes to her father in half an hour.

They started with the class rooms in the converted stable block. Taylor chose them because he knew that no other boys would be anywhere near them on a Sunday morning. It was a perplexing thought, but he realised that for some peculiar reason he didn't want to share this girl with anyone else until he really had to.

He talked as they walked along.

'I expect it's all a bit odd for you, coming to an all boys' school.'

'It's certainly different,' she said, 'but I'm really looking forward to it.'

'I hope you don't think too badly of the lads when you meet them,' he said. 'You just remember that boys can be a bit rough sometimes. But don't worry, I won't let them be nasty to you.'

She grinned. 'Oh, I think I'll cope. I shouldn't boast, I know, but my bro, he's 14, says I'm a better wrestler than most of the boys in his class at school. I won't mind getting in the odd fight.'

Had Ben told Taylor, the previous day, that he had heard Sam was a good fighter, the boy would have been shocked to the core that a girl could be like that. But now, as he walked happily beside her, his only thought was that she really was a frightfully good thing.

The tour continued, the conversation never flagging. Taylor had sometimes been forced into the company of girls when the family had visitors in the holidays and whenever that had happened he had found the experience deeply distressing. It was not that he didn't like them, it was just that he hadn't the faintest idea what to say to them. They were girls, not human beings. But the extraordinary thing now was that the words were flowing quite naturally. It was almost as if he were talking to Parsons or one of the other boys.

Little did he realise it, but a similar transformation had come over Sam. She had never been quite as tongue-tied in the presence of boys as Taylor had been with girls, but she had always felt more comfortable with other girls. Although she had genuinely been looking forward to going to a boys' school, she had also been nervous about it. And what had worried her most was whether she would be able to act naturally with boys and whether conversation would be easy, or horribly strained. Now, with this boy at least, she had found there was no strain at all.

It helped, of course, that Taylor was such a good-looking boy. While he remained in a state of total confusion about his reaction to her, she, being a girl, and therefore rather more mature, was well aware his physical appearance made him a particularly attractive companion.

On their way upstairs in the main building they had their first encounter with another boy. It was Mitchell Major. He had just spent twenty minutes listening to the chatter of boys, all determined that the arrival of a girl should not be allowed to change the ways of Portland, so, when he saw Taylor and Sam he thought it his duty to make clear his disapproval of her presence in the school.

'Off to play with some dolls are you, Taylor?' He grinned rather nervously as he spoke. Taylor was not usually a boy one would cross, but this was surely an exception. Anyway, he was hardly likely to retaliate when a girl was around.

Taylor's first thought was that he should give Mitchell Major a bloody nose, but a moment's reflection led him to the perfect reaction. He turned to Sam. 'Would you like to deal with this bounder, Watson, or shall I?' he asked.

She knew exactly what to do and say. 'Leave it to me, Taylor.' As she spoke, she raised her right hand, clenched her fist and let fly. Poor Mitchell Major had no chance. He tumbled backwards down the stairs (fortunately only three of them) and lay on his back looking up at a giant of a girl, fists still clenched, waiting for him to get up. Just as he was wondering how he should deal with this attack, a group of four boys came into the hall. He looked at Sam, then he looked at the boys, then he did the best he could. 'Jolly silly of me,' he said, 'I seem to have tripped over.'

Taylor grinned at Sam. 'Doesn't look like there's much for me to do. I hope you'll come to my rescue if I need some help.'

It was later, as they sat side-by-side on the bed in her room, that Taylor learnt something of the reason for Sam's arrival at Portland. As she explained it his imagination ran riot. What a chance for heroism, he thought, but little did he realise what adventures lay ahead.

'I don't know why,' she spoke hesitantly to start with, 'but I think I can trust you.'

'Of course you can.' He had long ago decided that he would gladly lay down his life for this amazing girl.

'OK, but this is top secret. Do you agree?'

'Cut my throat and hope to die.'

She took a deep breath. 'Right, only Mr Spencer knows this.'

She began her tale, and what a strange one it was. Taylor allowed her to tell it all. At the end he stared into her face, finally deciding that all she had said had been the truth.

As he absorbed it all, it dawned on Taylor that he now had a far more important duty than introducing a new pupil to the ways of Portland. He had to do all in his power to ensure that that new pupil remained safe. He prayed he would succeed.

Chapter 6

Matron Has a Drink

Taylor's pleasure at the prospect of teaching English to the junior boys was rapidly diminishing as the time for the first lesson approached. Ben had given him some tips on the topics he should be covering, but had consciously decided not to give any advice on the thing that was now concerning Taylor most. How was he, a 12 year old pupil, going to keep ten 8 and 9 year old boys in order?

Real masters, of course, had various weapons in their armoury which would simply not be available to him. Interesting though it would be, for instance, to be on the painless rather than the sore end of a gym shoe or cane, that was not an option. Neither, he feared, did he have a biting sarcastic wit ready to be deployed at a moment's notice. There was always the possibility of sending boys to a real master, but that just didn't come naturally to a proper English schoolboy; it was too much like sneaking.

The more he thought about it, the more nervous he became, and he knew that being nervous could result in disaster. There was nothing schoolboys picked up faster than nerves in a master. Once they had been spotted, the poor man's fate would be sealed. And that could happen to grown men. How much worse, he thought, it would be for a boy.

That Sunday night, he tossed and turned in bed as he wrestled with the problem. He was due to take the very first lesson on Monday morning and he realised he was terrified. Eventually, he did manage to get to sleep.

Thank goodness he did, because the answer came to him in his dreams.

At 8.30 sharp he stood outside the classroom and took a deep breath. He could hear the boys laughing and shouting on the other side of the door. That was not something they would have done if they had been expecting the arrival of a real master. No, they were clearly not intending to make life easy for him.

Just as he was about to open the door, Ben came into the corridor. For a moment, Taylor thought the master was going to silence the boys himself, but he was much too wise to do that. He just winked at Taylor and wished him good luck. He knew perfectly well that this was the boy's biggest test. To take it out of his hands would be the quickest way to guarantee disaster.

Taylor took another deep breath, then firmly gripped the door handle, turned it and strode into the room.

As he had expected, the noise only stopped for a second while the boys looked up to make sure the new arrival was not a proper master. Seeing it was Taylor, they happily resumed their chatter.

He stood for about ten seconds, staring at them. Then he slowly walked to the master's desk. He was gratified to note that the noise diminished as the boys wondered what he was up to. He had not made the classic mistake of immediately trying to shout them down. He pulled out the chair from behind the desk and climbed onto it (it was on the high side for a boy but he was tall enough not to look ridiculous). Then he gazed round the room, looking into each boy's face in turn, relieved, in particular, to catch Roberts's eye and to recognise, instantly, that the hero of the first form was on his side.

His heart was beating at an alarming rate. All depended on the next few seconds. Would they, as he prayed, stop talking, or would he have to command silence?

Gradually - it seemed to him to be taking hours but it really was only seconds - the chatter and giggles subsided. Soon there was total silence. The boys, he could see, were thoroughly perplexed.

He waited another few seconds then, hoping he was disguising his terror, he spoke. 'Right, lads, this is what happens. No one gets sent to a master. I'm not a sneak.' One of the boys started to cheer, but Taylor fixed him with an icy stare and he decided against continuing. 'No one gets detention.' It was working, they liked these announcements and were eager to hear more. There was a long pause. 'But,' the stare became icier, 'there's two sides to this deal. If you break your side of it, if you muck me around, you've broken the Portland code,' he paused again, 'and we all know what that means, don't we?'

The boys gasped in horror as the words sunk in. There was not one of them who did not understand. It was one of the first things a boy learnt on coming to the school. All prep schools have an unwritten code of honour. It forbids things like sneaking or failing to own up when such a failure will lead to an innocent boy being punished. To break such a code is to be guilty of about the worst sin any schoolboy could imagine. And the boy who does it will face a terrible fate at the hands of his peers. In the case of Portland, such a boy meets that fate in break, behind the cricket pavilion.

In fact, even in Taylor's four years at the school, no boy had actually been summoned to the cricket pavilion in break, but that was for the simple reason that the experience was such an appalling one to contemplate that no boy ever dared to break the code. And those ten boys being addressed by Taylor were now all secretly resolving never to put a foot wrong in his classes.

It had worked. Now for the lesson.

'Ok,' said Taylor, 'I want you to write an essay this morning.' There was a low groan from his pupils, but he ignored it. 'There'll be a prize for the best one. The title is: "Describe the Best Practical Joke to Play on a Master." Get writing.'

And that worked too. This was a topic dear to the heart of every normal prep school boy. As one, they picked up their pens and began scribbling.

Taylor was delighted he would not be meeting any of his young charges behind the pavilion in break. Indeed, it had dawned on him that he didn't actually know what happened to a boy behind the pavilion.

* * *

Ben, in the next classroom, had no idea how Taylor had silenced his charges but he was deeply impressed, as the first period went through to its conclusion, by the total absence of any sound.

* * *

Taylor had to make the instant transformation from master to pupil as the bell rang for the end of the first lesson. Having dismissed his class, not before exchanging conspiratorial winks with Roberts, he rushed to the other end of the corridor to join his own. He was hoping, desperately, although he could not have explained why, that Sam would be occupying the desk next to his. There were two free desks in the room, one next to Taylor's and one next to Parsons's. His delight was complete when he saw Sam sitting inches away from where he would be sitting.

Not for the first time, he marvelled at how odd it was that on some days everything seemed to go extraordinarily well, and on others nothing ever went right. This, clearly, was in the former category.

There was no real opportunity until after prep in the evening for Taylor and Sam to talk alone, but at last that moment came. Taylor had only heard the barest outline of her strange story and he longed to hear it all. Now was his chance.

He was entirely happy to risk the inevitable jibes that would follow from his decision to stay in a classroom with Sam rather than go to the common room with the other boys. Not only was he to be told an amazingly exciting and secret story, but he was also to be told that story by someone who was, he was astounded to acknowledge, becoming his best friend.

* * *

Meanwhile, Matron was about to make a new friend in the village pub having been quick to capitalise on the headmaster's decision to transfer nearly all her duties to Sarah. Now, instead of terrorising small boys getting ready for bed, she headed straight for the pub at opening time. As Taylor and Sam sat talking in the classroom, Matron was ordering her third gin and tonic of the evening.

She hadn't noticed the man in the camel hair coat standing at the bar., but now he spoke to her.

'Madam....'

She couldn't quite place the accent, not upper class, that was for sure, not really middle class either, but neither did it seem to be working class.

'.... I was wondering if you would permit me the honour of purchasing your drink for you?' Yes, that was it, used car salesman, that's what he must be. But there was no point in being stuffy about these things. A free drink is a free drink, wherever it comes from.

'That's very kind of you. Thank you very much.'

'Am I correct,' he went on, as the barman poured the drink, 'in thinking you are a member of the staff at that excellent educational establishment, Portland Court Preparatory School for Boys?'

Matron remembered Mr Spencer's solemn warning to them all not to get into idle conversation with strangers about the school. It was something to do with that girl, Watson. Honestly, what was the man thinking of, taking on a girl? It would only mean masses more work for her. At least the boys could be left in young Glossop's care in the evenings, but a girl required female supervision. Perhaps she should insist on a pay rise. Yes, that was what she would do.

Such thoughts had been going through her mind ever since Sam's arrival at the school, although it does have to be said that her only contact with the girl had lasted no more than thirty seconds. Now, as she recalled the silly instruction not to talk about the school just because of the girl, the thoughts rushed through her mind again.

'Well,' she sounded hesitant. She didn't want to disobey Mr Spencer's instruction, but neither did she want to be rude to this supplier of free gin and tonics, 'I suppose there's no harm in admitting it, yes, I am the school matron.'

The man seemed to detect her reluctance to be drawn and quickly changed the subject.

'I say, barman,' he said, 'do make that a double.' He turned back to matron. 'Allow me to introduce myself. Benjamin Marrow, at your service.'

Matron beamed in approval of his instruction to the barman. 'I am delighted to meet you, Mr Marrow.' She extended her hand. 'Mabel Stafford.'

Mr Marrow ordered himself a small pink gin and took both glasses to a table by the fire. When they had settled down, he returned to the subject of Portland Court but in a way which he hoped would overcome Matron's obvious concerns. 'I perhaps ought to tell you, Miss Stafford, that my interest in Portland Court is due entirely to the fact that I am at present engaged in attempting to find a suitable school for my son.' A look of sadness came over his face. 'We lost my wife, his mother, only three months ago and I have had to think long and hard about what I can do to bring some happiness and stability back to the lad's life. It seems to me, if you don't mind my saying so, good lady, that a small boarding preparatory school, with a dedicated matron, such as I feel sure you are, would be just the ticket.'

This new line worked a treat. Mr Spencer could have no objection to Matron talking about the school to a prospective parent, a supplier of fees.

'Oh, Mr Marrow, what a sad story,' she said. 'I won't pretend I am not overburdened with work already, what with our having added another pupil already this term, but I could never allow such considerations to lead me to dissuade a widower such as you from enrolling his son in the school.'

'I could tell, instinctively, madam, that you were just the sort of angel my boy needs.' Mr Marrow, if that really was his name, had detected that the gins she had already consumed had begun to have the sort of effect which allows wildly lavish compliments to be taken at their face value. 'But your glass is nearly empty. Please allow me to get you another.'

Half an hour later he successfully brought the conversation round to the new pupil to whom Matron had referred.

'I do hope that this other boy of whom you spoke, the one who has just arrived, does not have a similarly sad story as my own boy's.'

'Ash it happensh,' two more large gin and tonics had been consumed by now, 'itsh not a boy at all,' she hiccoughed, 'itsh extraordinary, but Mr Spensher, headmashter you know,' another hiccough, 'hash admitted a girl. Can you imagine such a thing, Mr Courgette?'

He interrupted, 'Do please call me Benjamin.'

'And you musht call me Mabel. I can't think what Mr Spensher was thinking about. Of course, he's not the one who has to look after the child. Oh no, itsh Matron who hash to work even harder than ever.'

Mr Marrow affected not to notice his companion's inebriated state. 'Is it not the same story everywhere, Mabel? Men have no idea how much work they demand of you selfless ladies. It must indeed be a great burden to find yourself charged with the care of a young girl, as well as all those boys. But how did it come about that anyone thought of sending a girl to the school?'

'I'm not sure I really know.' All caution was now gone. 'There sheems to be shome great secret about her. We're not even allowed to shay she's there, or that her name ish ... goodnesh I can't even remember her name. Itsh something like Holmes. No, itsh not Holmes.' She didn't notice that Mr Marrow was sitting on the edge of his seat. 'Itsh the name of that doctor who lives with Holmes. You know, Holmes the detective.'

'Dr Watson, you mean?' A strange and rather menacing smile flitted over his face.

'Thatsh the one, not that she's a doctor. Too young, you shee.' She fell back in her chair and closed her eyes, exhausted by the mental strain of trying to remember so much.

Mr Marrow smiled again, and started planning his next move.

* * *

Taylor had found it hard to take in all Sam had told him, but the bare bones were clear enough. Her father, it seemed was a man of great wealth who, despite his natural kindness and charm, had made some enemies in the course of building up that wealth. Men who had tried to cheat him, and failed, had now resolved to strike where they knew it would hurt.

The scheme they had hit upon was a dastardly one. Their plan was to kidnap his only daughter and to threaten her with dreadful tortures unless he paid them a large part of his fortune. An attempt had already been made at her previous school. Quite fortuitously, it had been foiled at the last minute, but the gang of crooks who had been hired for the job had got away. No one knew who they were, though Mr Watson had a pretty good idea who their paymasters were. She had now been moved, in what was hoped was secrecy, to Portland Court, the thought being that no one would ever imagine that a girl would be at an all boys' school. But the danger was ever present. The fiends might try again, at any time.

Once the full story had been told, Taylor swore to himself that he would be ever vigilant. He would save his damsel in distress and ensnare the evil kidnappers. Like Mr Marrow, but with a far higher motive, he started to make his plans.

* * *

It was Mr Green who took the call from the barman. It was not an unusual summons. With a heavy sigh he set off to collect a comatose matron from the village pub. He found her, sitting entirely alone at a table by the fire. He heaved her to her feet and managed somehow to carry her large bulk to the car.

He doubted whether they would see her at breakfast the next morning.

* * *

Mr Marrow was sitting on the bed in the room he had hired in the pub. He was grinning again as, at last, a plan came to mind. It would mean acquiring a boy to take with him up to the school, but that, he was sure, would not be beyond his abilities.

* * *

As Ben walked down the main staircase, having turned the lights off in senior dorm, he could tell once more that he was being watched. He hadn't had the feeling for several weeks.

He stopped and looked up, down, to the right and to the left. He could see nothing and no-one, but he was certain.

Chapter 7

Mr Marrow Appears

'Crikey, lads,' Parsons cupped his hand to his right ear, 'is it an earthquake?'

The three boys had all looked up as the thudding sound, which seemed to come from somewhere near the main hall, echoed round the common room.

As Parsons spoke, Taylor opened the door and walked in, a wide grin on his face.

'Hey, Taylor, what's all that row?' asked Parsons.

'It's only the elephant coming down stairs.'

'Did she roll down or something?'

'No,' Taylor's grin grew even wider, 'she ran.'

Mercer's jaw dropped. 'The elephant, running? Wow, that's a first. What's the hurry?'

'You'll never believe this, lads,' Taylor was now almost choking with laughter, 'but I reckon she's got a boyfriend. Some bloke she met in the pub. He rang up for her. The Tickler,' the boys' name for Mr Pine, 'sent me up to get her.'

Taylor's extraordinary ability to get to the bottom of everything is something at which all must marvel. He had just happened to be in the main hall when Mr Pine answered the telephone. All he had heard was the Tickler's side of a very brief conversation.

'I'll get a boy to get her for you.' That was it. Nothing more. Then he had called out to Taylor who had been about to set off for the common room. 'Hey, Taylor, be a good lad. Run upstairs and tell Matron there's a Mr Marrow on the telephone for her.'

How did he work out, from such little evidence, that Mr Marrow was a man Matron had met in the pub and that Mr Marrow was a man whom Matron fancied as her boyfriend? I don't know, but I do know that he did work it all out and all his suppositions were correct.

* * *

Matron was slightly out of breath after her unaccustomed run down the stairs but she composed herself before picking up the receiver.

'Good afternoon.' She sounded very much in control of her emotions, though her heart was beating rapidly as she wondered why Mr Marrow, Benjamin, should have telephoned her.

'Oh, Mabel – is it still permissible for me to call you "Mabel"?'

She looked round furtively to ensure that no prying boy or master was within earshot.

'Of course, Benjamin. I hope we are friends.'

'Indeed we are, Mabel,' he allowed a long pause and her heart beat even more wildly. Then his voice became more serious. 'I hate to impose on our friendship,' he began, 'but you may remember my mentioning Julius.'

Matron had no idea who Julius might be, but she was not going to admit her ignorance. She was remarkably fortunate in that, despite her frequent alcoholic lapses, her recoveries were never afflicted by feelings of guilt. If she couldn't remember what had happened after a few gins and tonics, she certainly didn't assume her amnesia had anything to do with the drinks. But she was sufficiently familiar with the problem to be aware that, once or twice, people felt they had mentioned things to her in bars that she didn't later remember. When that happened, she just assumed they were mistaken. In this case, she was quite right: Mr Marrow had never uttered the name "Julius", if only because he had only a moment ago thought it up.

'Of course, Benjamin, how could I forget Julius?'

She desperately tried to think what Julius might be - a cat, a dog, an aged grandfather? She just hoped the conversation might reveal more.

'Oh, Mabel.' He sounded so romantic. She sighed. 'I knew you would never forget my dear son.'

His son? How could he have a son? Did that mean he had a wife? She almost panicked, but then, wonderfully, she remembered. Of course, his wife had recently died. He had been left with a son, a prep school-aged son, for whom he was looking for a school.

'Yes,' she said quickly, eager to demonstrate how much she remembered, 'dear Julius. How is the poor boy?'

'He's bearing up. He misses his mother, bound to, but he's not a chap to give up. A chip off the old block, I dare say. He looks to the future.'

And so the conversation went on. Eventually Mr Marrow got to the point. He was sure Portland Court was the place for Julius. Did Mabel think that there might be the slightest chance that the school, which he was convinced would have a very long waiting list, might conceivably be able to make a space for his son?

Matron was very well aware that Portland Court would easily be able to accommodate another thirty or forty boys without trouble (except for the sort of trouble caused by masters complaining about having to do a bit of work), but she could see her cause might be better advanced by giving a rather different impression.

'Well,' she hoped she was sounding hesitant, 'I won't pretend it's that easy to get a boy in here, but what I will say, because I know what a deserving lad he is, is that I will do all in my power to persuade Mr Spencer to let him jump the queue.'

'Oh, Mabel.' There was something about the way he said her name - perhaps it was just because no one else ever said her name at all or perhaps it was because he was the only man for ages who had not addressed her as Matron – but whatever it was, she was suddenly sure she was in love. 'Oh, Mabel,' he said it again, 'I just knew I could rely on you. Let us strike while the iron is hot. Can I bring ....' There was a pause, she put it down to emotion, he, on the other hand, knew that it was that he had momentarily forgotten the name he had given to his "son", "... um, young, um, Julius, to see the school?'

She wondered whether, in order to give more credence to the notion that getting a boy into Portland Court was a tricky business, she ought to say that she would have to check with the headmaster, but she decided against it.

'A splendid idea. How about after church tomorrow morning?'

And so it was arranged. Mr Marrow's son, Julius, would pay a visit to the school on the following morning, a Sunday.

* * *

Mr Marrow's grin was an evil grin. He carefully replaced the receiver and turned to the quivering eleven year old boy standing by his side.

'Just remember, my lad,' he said, the grin still fixed on his face but a threat implicit in his tone, 'this is your chance to better yourself, to go up in the world.' He paused and the grin disappeared. 'And, lest you forget, put one foot wrong and your sister meets a terrible end.'

* * *

Mr Spencer was delighted by Matron's news. Really, everything was turning out wonderfully. Now that Taylor (a boy who needed no remuneration) had taken over one master's duties, the Watson girl had added to the fee income and Matron was introducing yet another fee paying pupil, life could not be better.

'Matron, this is splendid news,' he gushed at her, 'I shall have to think of a reward for you.'

Matron was quick to help his thinking process. She had by now convinced herself absolutely of the iniquity of the decision to admit a girl to the school. If she had given some honest thought to the matter, she would have admitted that Sam's arrival had made no difference at all to her duties. True, Sarah had found herself with even less time on her hands since the girl had come, but Matron had remained untouched.

It has to be said that Matron did not give any honest thought to the matter. She simply worked on the assumption that a girl pupil would be bound to lead to more work for a matron. She was already overworked, she had no doubt of that. This was the time to ask for a salary increase.

'Most kind of you, headmaster.' She hoped her smile was a charming smile (but it wasn't). 'I do have to say that I was wondering whether it was really right that I, as the only female member of staff, ought to take all the burden of looking after the Watson girl without any commensurate increase in my remuneration.'

Mr Spencer was not a stupid man. He knew full well that Matron's workload was astoundingly light. He knew Matron had done nothing at all to look after Sam Watson. He knew there was another female member of staff, Sarah, who was working a hundred times harder than Matron for less than half her pay. But he also knew there was something about Matron which parents found strangely comforting. Perhaps it was her enormous size. Whatever it was, there was no doubt that being able to parade Matron in front of parents always seemed to get a chap out of a sticky situation. So, though no one could say she actually merited better terms, it was as well to keep her on-side.

'Matron,' he said after a moment's thought, 'I am terribly conscious of the burdens we place on you. If there were more money in the pot I would have no hesitation in giving it all to you. But, sadly, especially with Mr Wilson's taxes, the money just isn't there.'

A dark look came over her face.

'But,' he rushed on, 'I do think we are working you too hard. I have decided you should be taken off morning duties.'

She almost smiled. It would have been nice to have a higher income but a reduction in working hours was hardly something at which one should sniff. And what was now proposed would mean she need have nothing to do with any of the boys (or that confounded girl) unless they were ill. Sarah had already taken over all bed time duties. Now, if mornings were to be matron-free, there was no requirement for her to see any of the pupils at all. There would still, of course, be the bore of coping with boys in sick bay, but that was not a major problem. For some reason which she simply couldn't fathom, the boys seemed very reluctant to admit to illnesses so severe as to require nursing from Matron.

* * *

Taylor was, unsurprisingly, chosen to escort young Julius Marrow around the school after church on the Sunday morning. As always, the boys (and one girl) walked back from the village in crocodile formation. As they got back to the school, they saw Mr Marrow (in his used car salesman's coat) and a boy standing near the main entrance. Mr Spencer was with them. Taylor and Sam were side by side. She knew he had to peel off to look after the prospective new boy.

As she got close enough to see the man and boy clearly, she suddenly gasped.

Taylor turned to her.

'What is it, Watson?'

She was lost for words for a moment, then she looked into Taylor's eyes.

'Is that the boy you're meant to be showing round?' she asked.

'I s'pose so.'

'What's his name?'

'Marrow, I think. Yes, Julius Marrow, that's it. Why?'

'Who's the man?'

'His father, of course. Look, what's the matter?'

She thought for a moment. Then she spoke again. 'I can't say now. I'll be in the classroom block when you take him there. We'll talk then.'

There was no more time for Taylor to investigate her concerns. He had to leave the line of pupils and join Mr Marrow, his son and the headmaster.

'Ah, Taylor, jolly good of you to help us out,' said Mr Spencer, who was somewhat relieved to find his star pupil coming to his rescue. 'This is Mr Marrow, and his son, um Marrow.'

'How do you do, sir,' said Taylor, proffering a hand to Marrow senior.

'Very well, I'm sure,' said Mr Marrow.

Taylor was far too well brought up to give any indication of his surprise at this odd response to his greeting. He smiled easily and, having shaken hands with the man, turned to the boy.

'Would you like a look around the place, Marrow?

Marrow senior gave what one might call a meaningful look at his "son". 'Yes, um, Julius, you run along with this nice lad, and,' there was a pause before he went on, 'remember all I said.'

The boy nodded dutifully. Taylor was slightly surprised at how nervous he looked, but then remembered that young Marrow might well be thinking he was about to be shown around a very frightening school.

As they set out on their tour, Taylor did his best to engage his charge in conversation but every response was no more than a grunt. He was beginning to think Marrow was not going to be a great addition to the school.

It was only when they got to the dormitories that Marrow came to life. It was as though he had suddenly remembered an instruction (which was actually the case). He took a deep breath and asked a question. 'I heard there's a girl here. Where does she sleep?'

So far, the boy had said nothing but 'yes' or 'no'. Taylor was astounded that he was able to produce two whole sentences.

'Oh, Watson you mean. Well, she's on the top floor, got her own room.'

The boy looked slightly quizzical as he heard the name "Watson", but he went on with his line of questioning.

'Can we see where her room is?'

Taylor was now thoroughly bemused. Why was this boy only interested in where Sam slept?

'Well, I suppose we can, if you really want to.'

They trudged up to the top floor and Taylor pointed out the door to Sam's room. Marrow stood for a moment, apparently getting his bearings, and then nodded, as though to say 'Ok, we can continue now'. He descended, once again, into silence.

At last, the two boys reached the class room block and visited two rooms before finally ending up in the one in which Sam was waiting for them.

Taylor noticed it the second they got into the room. Marrow's face turned instantly white.

Sam stared at Marrow. There was silence, but Taylor knew something very odd was happening.

It was Sam who spoke. 'What are you playing at, Tim?'

Taylor looked around. There was no one else there. Who was Tim? He looked at Marrow. The boy's complexion had changed again, this time from white to red. He was looking at his feet. He was clearly very disturbed.

'Come on, Tim,' Sam went on, 'what's this about?'

There was silence. Taylor stared at the boy and was horrified to see tears welling up in his eyes. This was definitely not the sort of boy one wanted at Portland Court.

At last, Marrow spoke. 'I just don't know, Sam,' he stammered through his sobs.

Taylor looked from boy to girl. Then, in exasperation, he spoke. 'Why are you calling him Tim?'

‘For the simple reason,’ at least she was calm, ‘that it’s his name. Tim Crane is his name, definitely not Julius Marrow’.

Taylor looked at the boy again. ‘Is that true?’

The boy sobbed again. But then looked up into Taylor’s eyes. ‘Yes. I’m not called Marrow or Julius or anything like that.’

‘Could someone,’ said Taylor, trying to be patient, ‘tell me what’s going on here?’

‘I hope,’ said Sam, ‘that that is just what Tim is going to do.’

There was another long silence. Then, having apparently made up his mind, Marrow (or Tim Crane) took a deep breath and started on his story. ‘It’s been awful. This Mr Marrow, he’s taken our spare room. Mum’s so happy to get the rent, but she doesn’t know what he’s like. He’s a beast, he really is. He made me come here today, pretending to be his son. He said I had to find things out, and, if I didn’t, he’d kidnap Lizzie and,’ he sobbed again, ‘torture her.’

Sam was nodding as though she could understand it all. Taylor was deeply perplexed. ‘What do you mean? What ‘things’ did you have to find out?’

‘He had to find out about me,’ said Sam. ‘That’s right, isn’t it, Tim?’

‘It must be,’ said Tim, ‘but I didn’t know it was you. He just said I had to find out all about the girl pupil at the school. I had to work out where her room was and then tell him. I swear, if I'd known he was talking about you, I'd never have done it, whatever he was going to do to Lizzie.'

A smile slowly came across Sam's face. 'What an idiot he must be,' she said.

'For goodness sake,' said Taylor, who had now worked out that this must be part of the plot to kidnap his young friend, 'how can you be so calm?'

'Easy,' she said, 'they've yet again employed twits to kidnap me. Honestly, fancy choosing a boy like Tim, a boy from the village, to do their spying for them. It hardly takes a genius to guess that any village boy would know me. That's where I live, for goodness sake.' She paused. Then she smiled again. 'It's obvious, I suppose. They think I'm a toff, because Daddy's rich, and so I won't know village children. That is just so incredibly stupid of them.'

Tim cheered up a little on seeing that Sam was not very cross with him. 'Yes, he's not very clever. I could see that.'

Taylor decided he had to show he was up to speed with all this. 'Right, um Crane, so this Marrow bounder, he's keen to find where Watson's room is so he can kidnap her from there.'

It was Tim's turn to look perplexed. 'Watson?' he asked.

'That's me,' said Sam. 'This is a boys' school, you see, so we're all called by our surnames.'

'Oh, yes, I see.'

'Anyway,' Sam continued, 'you've got it right, Taylor. This Marrow wants Tim here to tell him where my room is so he can creep up here one night and take me away. So, what are we going to do about it?'

At last Taylor felt the ball was back in his court. There were plans to be made and there was no one better at plans than Taylor.

He thought for a moment and then explained what they should do. 'First,' he started, 'whose room on the top floor is furthest away from yours, Watson?'

She smiled as she realised what he was going to propose. 'Matron's.'

'Exactly. So, Marrow, or Crane or whatever your name is, you will be telling Mr Marrow that Matron's room is the one he must head for.'

Chapter 8

Into Action

Taylor realised there wasn't time to make detailed plans. It was vital Tim should be got back to his "father" before suspicions were raised. But they agreed the basics. Tim would tell Mr Marrow Sam's room was Matron's. Beyond that, there was no need for him to say any more. Further plans could be delayed until the three could meet again, on the following Wednesday - a half day.

Both Sam and Taylor slept little on Monday and Tuesday. They were petrified Mr Marrow and his associates might strike early before the detailed plans could be made. But, fortunately, nothing happened before Tim crept back to the school on Wednesday afternoon.

It had been agreed they would meet behind the cricket pavilion, the place where Taylor would have had to administer justice to his pupils if they had been foolish enough not to buckle under. In an effort to conceal their movements from the whole school, Sam arrived first, Taylor arrived next and, ten minutes later, Tim joined them.

'Right,' Taylor had worked out his approach beforehand and was determined to take control, 'we've got to arrange a way of communicating. Any ideas?'

'I climbed onto our roof yesterday,' said Tim, 'and I could see the chimneys, up there,' he pointed to the top of the main building of the school on the eastern side. 'I could flash a torch, aiming it there, at night. Three flashes would mean nothing was happening, four would mean the raid was on. But would you be able to get up there, to see it?'

Taylor thought for a moment. 'Yes,' he said, 'I can get up there, but it'll be tricky. I can only risk it for five minutes. The best time would be ten o'clock. There are no masters around then, apart from gusset twanger, but he's always chatting up Miss Wilton in the masters' common room. But some of them start getting back from the pub at about half past. So it'll have to be ten o'clock exactly and the signals will have to be a bit more complicated. If all's ok, you do your three flashes, then wait for me to flash back three to show I've seen. Then you do three again. If there's trouble, do your four, then I do four and you do another four.'

Tim reported that Mr Marrow had been having secret discussions with another man, a Mr Turnip, who had taken a room in a neighbour's house. He, Tim, had not yet been able to eavesdrop, but he had every hope of being able to do so before long. He was pretty confident Mr Turnip was part of the conspiracy.

All three agreed, chiefly at Sam's instigation, that the police should not yet be alerted to what was going on.

'At my last school they told the police, and it was a disaster,' she said. 'They kept coming round to check up on things. All they succeeded in doing was showing we knew something was up. And then, when my housemistress told them she was suspicious about a man who turned up to ask about his daughter getting into the school, they sort of lay in wait for him. Of course, he was perfectly genuine. So, when they pounced on him and arrested him, there was an enormous fuss. They got frightfully embarrassed about their mistake and gave up completely. It was the purest luck I wasn't snatched away when the crooks made their real attempt.'

* * *

Tim had some interesting news when the three of them met behind the cricket pavilion a week later. There was no doubt Mr Turnip was part of the conspiracy. He had come to see Mr Marrow the previous evening. Tim had managed to get out of his usual washing up chore after high tea and had slipped upstairs, into the bathroom, which was next to Mr Marrow's bedroom, and listened, ear to the wall, to the conversation.

'It was amazing,' he whispered to his obviously enthralled audience, 'they were going into all these details about how they would do it. I mean, about how they would get you away from here.' He looked wide-eyed at Sam. 'They've got some kind of potion that makes people go to sleep. They said one of them would climb up a ladder to your room and get in through the window. Apparently they've heard that all boarding schools have a thing about windows being open at night 'cos it's good for you. Then he's going to give you the potion and wait for you to fall asleep and carry you down the ladder.'

Taylor grinned. 'They'll certainly get a shock when they find it's the elephant, not Watson.'

Tim looked perplexed for a second. He had not got used to the strange ways of Portland. He knew perfectly well that Sam's surname was Watson. It just didn't come naturally to him to use that surname rather than to call her Sam. He had also forgotten that Matron was known as 'the elephant', but his confusion was only momentary. He chuckled, 'Yes, I'd love to be there to see his face.'

'Well,' said Taylor, a note of determination in his voice, 'you may well be there. I'm going to need your help when they try it. We daren't tell any of the other lads what's going on yet. That means I'm going to need you here to help with our trap.'

'Oh no, Taylor,' exclaimed Sam, 'you can't put Tim in danger. We must cope with this on our own.'

But Tim was horrified at the suggestion he might be left out of the adventure. 'No, of course I must help. If it hadn't been for me agreeing to pretend to be Mr Marrow's son, none of this would have happened.'

'It's ok, Tim,' said Taylor, making it clear he had made the decision, 'you'll definitely be needed. Look, this is the plan.'

The three huddled closer as Taylor explained what they would have to do.

'The best thing, obviously,' he said, 'would be if we have advance notice of when they're going to strike. But we must assume the worst. Let's suppose we only get to know they're on the way when Tim gives his four flashes of the torch at ten o'clock. If that happens, he's got to run here straight away.' He fixed Tim with such a serious look that the poor boy almost felt like retiring from the whole exercise, but that idea only lasted for a moment.

'I know they'll be in a car,' Taylor went on, 'but you'll be able to cut across the fields, so you should be here very soon after them. Anyway, they'll be held up by finding they've got to the elephant's room, not Watson's. You must come to the kitchen garden door (I'll show you where that is). I'll be waiting there. Then we'll have to go upstairs and catch them in the act.'

'But you two can't take on two grown men.' Sam was beginning to wonder whether it might not even be better to involve the police than to leave everything to Taylor.

'True,' Taylor nodded his agreement as he spoke. 'The second I get Tim's signal, I'll get the other boys in senior dorm onto this. I know we'll need back-up troops, and they'll be up to it. But I'll need a decent lieutenant with me, and that has to be Crane.'

They continued their whispered plans for another half an hour. Both Tim and Sam were amazed at how Taylor seemed to have thought of every possibility. Having started their discussions worrying that they, two twelve year old children and one eleven year old, couldn't have any real chance of foiling the kidnappers' plot, they found themselves confident in their assumption all would be well.

* * *

For the next three weeks nothing happened other than the nightly exchange of three flashes of torches. Even Sam began to wonder whether the threat might be more imagined than real. But Taylor remained convinced there was a damsel in distress who would need saving.

Half term came. Sam was to go home to her father's house in the village. Taylor would, in normal circumstances, have been overjoyed by the news that his parents were going to give him a real treat by taking him to Harrogate for a week, but he hated the idea of leaving Sam so close to danger.

'Honestly, Watson,' he said to her a week before the holiday was due to start, 'I would much rather come and stay with you.'

'Oh, rot, Taylor,' she grinned, 'no one gives up a week in Harrogate. It's nearly as good as going abroad. I promise you, there'll be no danger. Daddy's even got an ex-policeman to come and protect us. You must go to Harrogate and have the most tremendous fun.'

Taylor gave in. And, of course, a holiday in Harrogate was not really something a boy of his age could contemplate sacrificing.

* * *

There was only one thing that happened in Harrogate with which we need to be concerned. It was on the Thursday. Taylor had gone out from the bed and breakfast house on his own. The sun had been shining when he had left but then there had been a sudden change. He had been a good half mile from their lodgings when the rain had started to pour down. He didn't really mind the thought of getting wet, but he knew his mother would be cross if he came back with his Aertex shirt and shorts absolutely drenched. So, when he saw a small hotel across the road, he decided to take shelter. He had nearly a shilling on him. That, he thought, should be enough to be able to overcome any difficulties. He would be able to buy a lemonade, at least. He darted in and looked around the lobby.

At first he didn't notice them. In fact, he was about to walk straight up to the reception desk to ask about the possibility of buying some refreshment. But, just in time, he spotted them. There, as large as life, were Mr Glossop "'gusset twanger") and Miss Wilton. They were walking from the staircase towards the reception desk. Half way across the lobby they were intercepted by a man who was obviously the hotel's manager.

'I do hope you enjoyed your stay with us, Mr and Mrs Smith.'

Taylor stepped backwards, hoping not to be seen.

'Indeed we did,' said Ben. 'We are just so sad to be leaving.'

Taylor knew instantly how important this was. Knowledge of this kind in an English prep school, was extraordinarily valuable. Of course, it could never be used for purely selfish purposes. There might be some cads who would try to avoid a caning by dropping in a casual reference to Harrogate, but Taylor was not that sort of boy. Nevertheless, knowing about "Mr and Mrs Smith" could one day be quite useful. And there was one thing Taylor knew perfectly well: any use his new-found knowledge might have would be quite lost if he shared it with any of the other boys. What he had seen and heard would remain secret until the moment arrived, if it ever did, at which it had to be deployed.

* * *

Taylor was enormously relieved to find, on his return to Portland, that Sam had also got back to the school. He was sorely tempted to tell her about what he had seen in that small Harrogate hotel but he stuck to his resolution. No one would find out about Mr Glossop and Miss Wilton from him, unless it became essential to release the information.

The next week passed without incident. Religiously, every night, Taylor climbed onto the roof and exchanged torch flashes with Tim. And, every night, no more than three flashes would be seen from the village.

But then, after eight days, it happened.

Taylor took his place by the chimneys. He waited. He saw one flash, then a second, then a third. He was about to give his own three flashes in return. But he waited a moment and kept his gaze directed at the torch half a mile away. Thank goodness he did.

There was a fourth flash.

For a second he felt a sort of elation. At last, the moment had come. But then he realised how serious this was. Sam was in danger and only he could save her. He shivered, though it wasn't cold. He gave his four flashes in return and then, after Tim gave another four, he scrambled down again. He had to get his troops organised.

* * *

Back in the village, Tim climbed down from the roof and started tiptoeing down the stairs. His mother was, he knew, in the sitting room, listening to the wireless. It would be a disaster if she came out and saw him trying to leave the house. Mr Marrow had left half an hour ago. Every moment would count. He winced as he heard the creaking of the floor boards but he crept on. Once he was down in the hall he heard his mother laugh. That was a good sign. She would be listening to the *Goons Show*. She would never stray far from the wireless when that was on. He got to the front door. It made a horrid screeching sound as he opened it. He turned back, holding his breath, to see if the sitting room door would open. It didn't. He slipped out and prepared for his sprint across the fields.

* * *

Meanwhile Mr Marrow and Mr Turnip were setting up their ladder underneath Matron's window.

Mr Marrow, no, let us give him his true name, Bert Jones, told Mr Turnip, Jeff Porter, that he, Bert, would climb the ladder. Jeff was to stay at its foot and wait for their "parcel" to be handed down to him. Slowly Bert ascended the ladder. All was silent. All was going according to plan.

* * *

Tim, horribly out of breath, ran across the cricket pitch. The moon was bright and the sky cloudless, but he couldn't see Bert and Jeff because they were on the other side of the house. Panting, he arrived at the walled kitchen garden. The gate, to his relief, was unlocked. He made his way in.

* * *

Bert got to the top of the ladder. The window was just ajar. It was not, as he had expected it to be, wide open, but at least it wasn't locked. He eased it up, took a deep breath and manoeuvred himself in, landing with a crash on the floor. The room was in darkness. He picked himself up and tried to work out where the bed was. He heard a groan from somewhere to his left. He turned. A light came on. For a second he was blinded, then the groan turned into a voice.

'Oh, Benjamin.' There was a pause. It seemed to last an age. What had happened? Was the school's matron tending to the girl? Was she ill? That was all he needed.

When he recovered his sight, he saw that the bed was occupied, not by a slight girl, but by a very large woman. She was lifting herself up.

'Oh, Benjamin,' she said again, 'this is so wrong, but I can forgive you. I feel as strongly for you as you do for me. I understand your passion. Come to me, dear Benjamin, come to me.'

Bert was not the quickest thinking of men but he worked out exactly what had happened. For some reason, he had got into Matron's room, not Sam's. For a moment or two he stood staring at her, wondering how he could escape, then he remembered the fee he would be paid if he succeeded in his mission. Somehow he had to get away from Matron and find the Watson girl.

How was he to do it?

He looked around the room and his eyes alighted on a half empty bottle of gin on a table by the door. That, he smiled to himself, was the answer.

'Oh, Mabel,' he hoped he sounded as passionate as she obviously expected him to be, 'I just couldn't keep away from you. Do you hate me?'

'Oh,' it was almost a wail, 'how could I? We were made for each other. What you want of me now is what I want of you.'

He hoped he disguised his shudder.

'But,' she went on, 'you know we mustn't do it, not here, not now.'

He let out a sigh of relief. He trusted it sounded like a sigh of disappointment.

'Oh, Mabel,' he thought he was getting quite good at this, 'I know you're right but I simply had to see you again. Let us at least have a little drink together.' He looked again at the bottle of gin.

If the truth be told, Matron was not entirely pleased with the speed at which he had given up on his amorous plans but she was never one to turn down an excuse for a drink.

'Of course, Benjamin, we can at least do that.' She pointed to the ledge above her wash basin. 'There are the glasses.'

He walked towards the basin and picked up the two thick tumblers. One, he saw with something approaching horror, contained what were obviously her false teeth. He put that one back and took the other to the table.

'Here, let me pour yours first,' he said.

He stood with his back to her as he poured a generous measure of gin into the glass and, unnoticed by her, tipped half of a small bottle of some other clear liquid (his "potion") into the tumbler as well.

'Is there any tonic, Mabel?' he asked, as he turned back to her.

'No, Benjamin, I'm afraid not, but water will be fine.'

He went back to the basin and turned on the cold tap. He put a tiny slurp of water into the glass and took it over to her.

She gazed lovingly into his eyes as she took the drink but, after only a couple of rather large gulps, felt strangely drowsy. She tried as hard as she could to remain sitting in her bed but will power was not enough. Slowly she sank back onto her pillow. Bert had to act quickly before she became completely comatose.

He knelt down by the bed and whispered into her ear. 'Oh,

Mabel, I want you so much but it's too dangerous here. Didn't you say there was that girl on this floor?'

She had never said a word to him about where Sam's room was but she was not in a state to doubt his word.

'Oh yes, the Watson girl,' she said, 'nothing but trouble, and it's me who has to cope with her.'

'You poor thing.' He was terrified she would fall asleep before he could get the information he so desperately needed. He would have to be direct. 'I just don't want to do anything if she might hear what's going on. Where's her room?'

He held his breath. Would she be suspicious at such an odd question?

Fortunately, she wasn't. 'It's just miles away,' she yawned.

'But where?' he prayed she would not detect the note of desperation in his voice.

Her eyelids started to close but she just managed to answer the question.

'Far end of the corridor. Last door on the right.'

Her eyes closed. She was dead to the world.

Bert took the tumbler of gin from Matron and poured its contents into the basin. Filling it with water, he added the remainder of the potion, then, as quietly as he could, he opened the door, looked out to make sure the way was clear, and headed down the corridor.

* * *

Taylor crept into senior dorm. Most of the boys were already asleep. They had to be woken but it would be fatal to his plans if waking them also alerted Gusset Twanger to his activities. He closed the door and made his way to each bed in turn. His heart was beating furiously but he knew he had to stay calm. If the Gusset Twanger appeared, precious minutes would be lost in explanation. Fortunately, the natural reaction of most 11 and 12 year old prep school boys on being woken in their dorms is to be silent. Taylor only had to hold his hand over two mouths. After five minutes his team of ten troops was alert and ready for action, though still wholly ignorant of the menace to be faced.

They silently made their way towards the stairs. All depended on timing. Taylor had no idea Marrow was already in the house and making his way towards Sam's room. Had he known, he would have thrown caution to the wind and ordered half his army to rush outside and the other half to go to Sam's room. But he didn't know. He assumed – and how wrong he was - that the car containing

Messrs Marrow and Turnip would only have set off a few minutes earlier. He thought time was on his side. He told the other boys to wait at the top of the stairs while he went down to meet Tim by the kitchen door.

* * *

Tim got to the back door of the house. He was just about to open it when he heard the sound of a man coughing slightly to his right. His first thought was that he had stumbled across Mr Marrow and his friend, but, in a moment, he realised he hadn't. A man of about forty suddenly lurched out of the shadows towards him.

'What on earth are you doing, boy?' the man demanded.

Tim couldn't immediately think of an answer to the question.

'I said, boy,' the man's voice sounded slurred, 'what on earth do you think you're doing?'

Tim found his voice. 'Oh, just walking,' he said.

'For goodness sake,' the man was now only inches away from him and staring down into his face. There was a smell of stale beer on his breath, 'it's long past lights out.' He paused. Then, with a note of steely resolution, he hoped, in his voice, he continued, 'I shall have to cane you.'

Tim couldn't disguise his relief. This was no kidnapper; It was a schoolmaster.

'Oh, you can't do that,' after a moment's pause he added 'sir'.

'Don't talk nonsense, boy, of course I must cane you.'

'But you can't, sir. I don't go to this school.'

'I won't stand for this,' said the man, stumbling slightly as he stepped towards the door, as though to make his point, 'we will go inside, find a cane, and get the whole business over and done with.'

* * *

Taylor reached the kitchen garden door. His hand was on the knob, ready to turn it, as he heard the voices outside. He froze. He couldn't make out what they were saying, but he knew he must wait.

He stepped back, ready to make a run for it if the voices belonged to the kidnappers.

* * *

Bert was thoroughly relieved to find Matron's information was correct. The light in the corridor was sufficient to show him that the sleeping child in the bed was Sam. He crept towards her, tumbler in hand. She stirred slightly as he got to her. Gently, surprisingly gently for such an evil man, he lifted her head and placed the glass to her lips. She was not fully awake. It was pure instinct that made her drink the liquid. It was only after she had taken several gulps that she took in who it was who was by her bed. She gasped in horror but it was too late. Bert clasped his hand to her mouth to stop her shouting out. In minutes, she was falling back, asleep again.

* * *

As Bert made his way back down the corridor, Sam balanced over his shoulder, Taylor stared in horror at the sight of Tim and an obviously tipsy Mr Pine (the 'Tickler') walking through the kitchen garden door.

'Not another boy out of bed,' said Mr Pine as he saw Taylor, 'I suppose I shall have to cane you as well.'

'Oh, hello, sir, how nice to see you,' said Taylor, trying to think how he could cope with this unexpected complication. Then he looked at Tim. 'How long have we got?'

'It's too late,' said Tim. 'They set off half an hour before the signals.'

Mr Pine looked from one boy to the other. 'What are you talking about, boys?'

'Oh, nothing to worry you, sir,' said Taylor, who now seemed to be back in control. 'I should go and have a snooze in the masters' common room if I were you. I'll look after Tim.'

'I shall certainly go to the masters' common room, Taylor, because that's where the canes are.'

Taylor ignored him and turned back to Tim. 'Do you know what their plan is?'

Tim was immensely impressed by Taylor's fearless treatment of the master and found it gave him some unexpected courage. 'Yes, I heard it all. They're taking her to Marlbury, to something they called a "safe house".'

'Do you know the address?'

'Stop this nonsense at once,' said Mr Pine, in exasperation, 'we are going to get a cane.'

'No, sir, we're not,' said Taylor in a tone Mr Pine found rather disconcerting. 'You can't beat Tim because he isn't a Portland boy. You can beat me if you wish to but you will have to wait a while. We have a matter of life and death to deal with first.' Mr Pine opened and shut his mouth, but no words emerged. Taylor turned once again to his trusty lieutenant. 'Do you know the address?' he repeated.

'No, I only know it's in Marlbury. But that's miles away. They've got a really fast car, a Rover, we'll never be able to find the house.'

Taylor grinned. 'Oh yes we will. It's miles by road, but it's just across the river. We've got the school's canoes. We'll be there long before them.'

'I will not stand for this,' Mr Pine's voice had now become strangely high pitched as he determined to re-impose his authority, 'I am going to thrash you two boys and then you're going to bed. Come with me to the masters' common room now.'

Taylor smiled sympathetically at the master. 'Very well, sir, we will accompany you to the masters' common room but only because we need Mr Glossop's help, and he should be there. Oh, by the way, sir, would you mind standing in for him as duty master for an hour or two, just till he gets back? You see, we need him to drive to Marlbury and pick up Watson's father on the way. I'd ask you to do it for us but I think you may be a bit too tired'

Once again poor Mr Pine was left speechless but at least, Taylor seemed to be agreeing to go to the masters' common room. That was a victory of sorts. So rather than continuing the argument he started on his rather uncertain walk in that direction.

* * *

Bert eased himself and Sam out through the window, smiling at Matron's loud snoring. Very slowly, he went down the ladder. At the bottom, Jeff started to ask why it had taken so long.

'There's no time for that.' Bert insisted. 'Let's be off.'

They left the ladder where it was and dashed for the Rover.

Jeff put the car into gear and set off down the drive. No one heard them drive away.

* * *

Mr Pine, Taylor and Tim walked into the masters' common room together. As the door opened, Ben and Sarah, who had been sitting rather closely together on the sofa, jumped apart.

'Ah, Glossop,' said Mr Pine, 'sorry to bother you old chap, but I need to cane these boys.'

'It's all right, sir,' said Taylor, looking quite in control of things, 'he doesn't really, but we do need your help with something.'

Ben could tell instantly that his colleague was inebriated. Even if that had not been the case, however, he would have paid more attention to Taylor than to Mr Pine.

'What is it, Taylor?' he asked.

'I haven't got much time to explain, sir, but we need you to drive to Marlbury and pick up Watson's father on the way. Mr Pine will take over as duty master while you're away.'

'Oh, come on, Taylor, I can't just go on a country drive when I'm in charge of all you boys. What's all this about?'

'It's to do with Watson, sir. She's been kidnapped and we know they're taking her to Marlbury. A few of the lads and I will take canoes across the river to get there before the crooks and see what house they're taking her to, but we'll need some grown-ups to help us when we've found the place.'

Even Ben found this difficult to take.

'Really, Taylor, you mustn't let these fantasies run your life. Go back to bed and we'll sort it all out in the morning.'

Taylor knew he had no alternative. Time was too short. His secret knowledge had to be used. He took a deep breath and spoke the only words he could think of which would do the trick.

'I really do think, sir, that you should help us. Harrogate is such a nice place to spend half term. I know Mr and Mrs Smith simply loved it.'

Ben and Sarah instinctively turned to look at each other. Mr Pine, who had long ago given up any thought of caning Taylor and Tim, wondered if he might indeed have had too much to drink. Tim shook his head in bewilderment.

Ben knew he had no choice. If his half term adventure with Sarah were to be revealed, Mr Spencer would have no alternative but to dismiss him. The parents would never stand for that sort of thing. He agreed to go on Taylor's ludicrous expedition.

Chapter 9

Taylor to the Rescue

Taylor was anxious. Too much time had already passed. It was vital that he and his fellow boys should start their crossing as soon as possible. He also needed Ben to set off without further delay.

'I'm sorry, sir, but I think you really need to get going.' He turned to Sarah. 'If you don't mind, ma'am, I reckon it would be a good idea if you went with Mr Glossop in the car. Watson's pretty tough, for a girl, but I'm sure she'd like you to be there to look after her when we free her.'

Neither Ben nor Sarah sought to argue with Taylor. The boy had taken command and they both knew him well enough now to go along with his plans.

Mr Pine, however, whose mind was still somewhat befuddled by the beer, was having great difficulty in following what was happening.

'Look, Glossop old chap,' he said, 'would you mind explaining what's going on? There I was, coming back from an evening walk, when I stumble across these two boys, long past lights out. It's obvious they need to be caned, but now you seem to be ganging up with them to go on some mad enterprise involving canoes and cars. I just don't understand it at all.'

Ben's only reservation was his reluctance to leave the rest of the boys in the charge of Mr Pine. The fact the older master continued under the impression that Tim was an errant Portland boy did not do anything to inspire confidence. On the other hand, there was no one else around, except perhaps Matron, who could keep an eye on things while Ben was away. As he wrestled in his mind with what he should do, Taylor, again, stepped into the breach.

'Sorry, sir,' he said to Mr Pine, 'but there just isn't time to explain it all now. We're all really grateful to you for taking over as duty master. Unfortunately, I expect the juniors will have woken up by now. But, don't worry, I'll have a word with them before we set off. They won't be any trouble to you.'

Yes, thought Ben, that was the best that could be done. Taylor's ability to control the juniors was well known. With any luck, whatever he said to them before he set off would do the trick.

But Mr Pine was still confused. He was beginning to get the idea that his authority was being challenged. Surely, he thought to himself, he should put his foot down. He attempted to jump up from the armchair in which he had slumped. Things weren't helped by his getting the manoeuvre wrong, but the others waited patiently while he picked himself up from the floor.

'Well,' he was addressing Taylor, 'I won't pretend I know what on earth is going on, but one thing is for certain and that, young man, is that I am going to cane you.'

Taylor didn't seem at all put out by this news. He smiled, as might a man eager to humour the village idiot. 'I'm frightfully sorry, sir, but that's going to have to wait. Don't worry, though, I'll be back later and you can do it then. Right,' he turned back to the others, 'let's go.' He strode to the door, opened it and ushered Ben, Sarah and Tim out before nodding a farewell to Mr Pine and leaving the room himself.

Poor Mr Pine. He had the distinct impression that he had come out of this rather badly. He looked around the empty room wondering, not for the first time, whether he was really cut out to be a school master. Then he saw the sherry bottle. Yes, that was the answer. That would get him through the evening.

* * *

Having despatched Ben and Sarah to the car, Taylor and Tim bounded upstairs to the first floor landing where the other troops were still waiting.

'Has anyone checked Watson's room?'

Parsons stepped forward. 'Yes, Taylor. I'm afraid she's gone. Goodness knows how they got her out. There isn't even a drain pipe running up the wall there.'

'Probably brought a ladder,' said Taylor 'Anyway, I expect they came in at the elephant's window.' He was recalling the false information Tim had passed to Mr Marrow. 'I'd better go and check she's ok. The rest of you, I want you to go down to the boat house and get out enough canoes for us. I'll join you as soon as I can.'

He took the stairs up to the second floor two at a time and ran along the corridor to Matron's room. The door was shut. He was tempted to burst in, so keen was he to get going, but good manners prevailed. He knocked.

There was no reply. He knocked again, louder. There was still no reply. He had no choice. He turned the handle and walked in. The bed side light was still on and the window was wide open. To his right he heard Matron's intermittent snores coming from her bed. He walked to the window. Sure enough, there was the ladder and, caught on a nail in the window sill, there was a fragment of Sam's pyjamas.

He turned to the bed. Had that woman slept through all this?

And how had Marrow known where to find Sam? He had to find out what Matron knew. He stepped forward and shook her by the shoulders. This was not a time for gentleness and, regrettably perhaps, he used all his strength.

She stirred. Her eyes opened, but they were not yet seeing eyes.

'Oh, Benjamin,' she sighed.

Taylor knew that Mr Marrow called himself "Benjamin". It suddenly dawned on him that the elephant had actually seen and spoken to Marrow. A look of steel came across his face. Had she been the fiend's accomplice? He would find out.

He leant towards her face. He could smell the gin. He grimaced and then he spoke loud and clear.

'It's not Benjamin Marrow, Matron, it's Taylor.'

She blinked and looked at the twelve year old boy bending over her bed.

'Taylor,' she exclaimed in astonishment, 'what are you doing, boy? This is disgraceful. Mr Spencer will hear about this.'

'Mr Spencer,' Taylor's voice was as steely as his expression, 'is going to hear a lot, Matron, like how you permitted a vile kidnapper to climb into your bedroom, how you told him where to find his victim and then, when he had stolen her away, how you calmly went back to sleep. Oh yes, Mr Spencer is going to be thoroughly shocked.'

Matron opened and shut her mouth. No sound came out. She honestly had no idea what Taylor was talking about but the sound of his voice sent a chill to her heart.

Finally she managed to speak. 'What do you mean, Taylor?' she no longer sounded belligerent. 'What kidnapper? What victim? What are you talking about?'

Now it was Taylor's turn to be confused. It was plain to him that she really didn't know about the kidnapping. Perhaps she had slept through it all. But then he remembered her waking words: "Oh Benjamin". She must have seen him.

'I'm talking about Mr Marrow climbing up here, up that ladder,' he pointed to the window, 'asking you where Watson's room was, going there, drugging her, carrying her back here and down the ladder.'

Matron went white. How did the boy know that Benjamin had come to see her? How did he know, as she now remembered, that Benjamin had wanted to know where the Watson girl's room was? And what did he mean by saying Benjamin had drugged Sam and taken her down the ladder?

A thought suddenly struck Taylor as he watched the frightened and puzzled expression on Matron's face.

'Did he give you something to drink?' he asked.

In normal circumstances, if one of the boys had asked her such an impertinent question he would have got a sharp answer, but Matron was too scared now. And, anyway, the same thought had struck her. If Marrow had drugged Sam, might he have drugged her too?

She nodded. 'Yes, in a tooth mug. And then,' her head sagged as she realised the truth, 'I went to sleep. I don't know anything about Watson. I promise you that.'

Tears were filling her eyes. Taylor didn't have time to marvel at the sight but he recognised her genuine anguish and allowed his expression to soften.

'Don't worry, Matron, we've got a pretty good idea where they're taking her. We'll get her back.'

'But how can you?' she gasped through the sobs, 'they're bound to have a car.'

Taylor smiled. 'Yes, but we've got canoes. Their safe house is just across the river. It'll take them an age to get there. It'll only take us minutes. I must go now.' Without more, he turned back to the door and hurried out.

He stopped on the first floor and went into junior dorm. As he had expected, the twenty boys were all wide awake, obviously wondering what was going on but not yet confident enough to investigate. He spoke to them for no more than thirty seconds. The words 'Portland Code' and 'stay in the dorm' were all that was needed. Then he dashed out and down the stairs.

* * *

Matron struggled to take it in. but slowly, she worked it all out. How could she have been such a fool? She remembered all his questions in the pub. He had kept going back to the subject of the Watson girl. He must have been milking her for information right from the start so that he could kidnap the poor girl, and she had happily answered every question. She had even - she shuddered as she thought it - told him where Sam's bedroom was.

For a few minutes she allowed tears of remorse to pour down her cheeks, but then anger took its place. She pulled her sheet up to her face, wiped away the tears and stared straight ahead with a look of icy determination. She pushed aside the bedclothes, grabbed a skirt, blouse and jersey and pulled them on.

She had run down the stairs at quite a pace when Marrow had telephoned. She now ran even faster. As she passed junior dorm, its occupants hid their heads under their blankets at the extraordinary sound. It was as though there was a thunder storm on the staircase.

She charged on. Nothing would stop her now. She must make amends for her stupidity. Most of all, she must wreak her vengeance on Marrow.

* * *

Sam began to stir in the back of the car. Jeff Porter ('Mr Turnip') was driving. Bert Jones ('Mr Marrow') was sitting in the back with Sam. As he saw her move, Bert quickly placed a large hand over her mouth.

'No-one's going to hurt you,' he said, in a tone so menacing as to give the lie to the words. 'If you're sensible and, more to the point, if your Dad is sensible, you'll be home again in days. But,' and here his voice dropped to an icy whisper, 'if you give us any trouble, you'll bitterly regret it.'

Sam's heart was pounding at an alarming rate but she was determined not to show her fear. She narrowed her eyes and, as he slowly moved his hand from her mouth, she answered him in what she prayed sounded a confident and fearless tone.

'All I can say, Mr Marrow, or whatever your real name is, is that any regretting that's going to be done won't be by me.'

Bert let out a low, evil sounding chuckle. 'We'll see,' he said, 'now keep quiet.'

* * *

Taylor was almost out of breath as he arrived at the boat house. He saw his troops had carried out their orders. Five two-boy canoes were lined up on the river bank. As he looked at the waiting boys, he wondered for a second whether he ought to send them back to get changed from their pyjamas and dressing gowns but he decided against it. He didn't know precisely when Sam had been taken and every minute counted.

'Ok, lads, pair up, get in your canoes and set off.' He turned to Tim, 'you come with me, Crane. We can perfect our plans on the way.'

Tim was now getting used to Taylor's insistence on using surnames. Indeed, if the truth be told, he was grateful not to be marked out as different from the other boys.

'Ok, Taylor, but I ought to tell you I have never paddled a canoe before. I've done quite a bit of rowing but never had a canoe.'

'Don't worry, just do what I do and you'll be all right.'

Being so close to its mouth, the river was tidal at the point of their intended crossing. It would have been better, Taylor thought, if it had not been high tide. The crossing would be a fair bit longer than at low tide but at least it seemed to be at its highest point. That should mean that they wouldn't be dragged up or down stream.

One by one the five canoes were placed in the water and the boys climbed in. Taylor detailed Parsons and Barker to lead. He and Tim would take up the rear. He wanted to be sure he could keep all the other boats in his sight in case of accidents.

'I just pray she's ok,' said Tim. 'I could never live with myself if she gets hurt.'

'Don't worry,' said Taylor, hoping he sounded as though he meant it, 'it's not in their interests to harm her.' Then, thinking a change of subject would help, he giggled and said, 'Poor old Tickler - that's Mr Pine, the master you bumped into. I hope the juniors don't give him too much trouble; he'll never be able to cope if they do.'

'I thought you were really brave the way you were so calm when he kept saying he was going to cane you. He won't really do it will he, when you get back?'

Taylor laughed again. 'Highly unlikely. To start with, he probably won't remember any of it when he wakes up in the morning. Or, if he does, he'll just think he imagined it all because he'd had too much beer in the pub. Anyway, it doesn't matter if he does go ahead and cane me. He's not called "the Tickler" for nothing.'

Tim was surprised at how quickly he had picked up the art of paddling a canoe. His nerves had left him and he was quite content chatting to Taylor as they made their way across the river.

'So, why is he called the Tickler?' he asked.

'Well, he's a curious chap really, for a school master. He's terrified of getting things wrong all the time. You know, in masters' meetings and things like that, he hardly ever speaks in case he might upset the head or another master. Anyway, we all found out quick enough that he's just as frightened that he might overdo it with the cane. First time he swished a chap - it was Parsons actually - we all wanted to know, obviously, how hard he was. Parsons came back to the common room looking really glum as though he was fighting back the tears. He said it had been awful, real agony. Then he sort of paused before grinning and saying, "it was as bad as being tickled by a chicken feather". So everyone started calling old Pine the Tickler.'

Tim chuckled. 'So, how does he keep order?'

'Of course, he just can't. His lessons used to be a riot from beginning to end but then a few of us realised we had to sort things out. After all, the last thing you want is to lose a master whose swishings are like being tickled. So I called a meeting of all the boys and told them it would be silly to muck around so much that the

Tickler had to leave. Most of the lads could see the point and they agreed to go easy on him. One or two went on ragging him but that soon stopped after I dished out some bloody noses.'

Although Tim had only met Taylor a very few times, he was already getting the impression, correctly, that Portland Court would simply collapse without the twelve year old being there to keep everything running smoothly. Tim marvelled at his new friend's qualities. To be frank, Taylor had rapidly become his hero.

There was a sudden splashing sound behind the boys. Both turned to look. The moon was bright and they could still see the Portland bank of the river quite clearly. It took no time to work out the cause of the sound. There, very low in the water, was a two boy canoe occupied by one person. The person, who seemed to be overflowing from the cockpit, was none other than Matron, the elephant.

'Oh no,' exclaimed Taylor, 'that's all we need. We're going to have to do an awful lot of silent creeping around tonight. The elephant's bound to make a frightful din.'

He thought of trying to signal to her to go back but he could see, as she got closer, that there was a look of such extreme determination on her face that it would be fruitless to do so. He would just have to try to keep her under control.

* * *

Ben and Sarah were both nervous as they knocked on the door of Sam's father's imposing house. There were no lights on downstairs, though there were a couple on in first floor rooms. They hoped Mr Watson had not already gone to bed. It was going to be bad enough telling him his daughter had been kidnapped and that a rescue mission had been mounted by a twelve year old boy, whose orders everyone else was obeying. To have to get their message across to a bleary eyed man who had just been woken from deep sleep would be almost impossible.

They heard footsteps in the hall. A moment later the door swung open and they saw, to their relief, that Sam's father was still fully dressed. He took only a second or two to realise who his visitors were.

'Oh God,' he said, 'Sam's been kidnapped, hasn't she?'

Ben nodded. 'I'm afraid so, sir,' he said, 'but we think we know where they're taking her. There's a village boy, Tim Crane is his name, who's got hold of some information.'

'Right,' said Mr Watson, 'where does he say they're keeping her?'

'Marlbury.' said Ben, 'We don't know exactly where in Marlbury, but one of the boys is taking a party of lads across the river in canoes.' Ben paused for a second as he wondered how Mr Watson would react to being told that it was boys, not masters, who were heading for Marlbury, but he knew he had to plough on. 'They should be there before the car taking Sam.'

To his credit, Mr Watson made no remonstrance at this news. Instead, he just asked one question.

'This boy you refer to. What's his name?'

'Taylor.'

Mr Watson smiled. 'Excellent. Sam's told me all about him. By all accounts, if he's in charge we should stand a pretty good chance of foiling the plot. Can I come in your car?'

Ben already knew enough about Mr Watson to understand he was both very intelligent and a man of action, but he was amazed, and very pleased, to see how quickly the tycoon had grasped all the facts and had known exactly what was required of him.

'Yes, of course,' said Sarah. 'We don't know how much of a start the crooks had over us but, with any luck, the boys'll be able to lead us to them once we get to the village.'

* * *

The five canoes forming the main part of Taylor's armada had been silently pulled from the water and hidden behind bushes on the Marlbury side of the river. The boys watched anxiously as Matron's canoe, now almost completely submerged as a result of her weight, inched its way towards them. With a few yards still to go, Taylor waded in so as to be able to pull the boat up the bank. He got to it just in time and, with almost superhuman strength, somehow managed to pull the enormous weight clear of the water.

Matron herself succeeded in squeezing her massive frame out of the canoe and collapsed, panting for breath, into one of the bushes. Just as Taylor had dreaded, the sound seemed to echo throughout the village.

A moment later they heard the unmistakable sound of a slightly squeaky bicycle on the road above the river bank. Taylor signalled for the boys to crouch down behind the bushes. Matron was already down there, in the process of trying to heave herself up. Taylor waved at her frantically, desperate to persuade her to stay still and silent. She sank back again. The sound was, again, at least to Taylor's ears, deafening. The bicycle stopped. It was obviously just above where they were hiding. Then a voice could be heard.

'Hello, hello, hello. What've we got here?'

Taylor sighed - a village bobby. And surely any policeman who actually said 'Hello, hello, hello' was hardly likely to be the brightest spark. They would have to get rid of him, and fast.

Taylor whispered to the others, 'Leave this to me,' and climbed up the river bank to confront the constable.

Once on the road, Taylor smoothed his dressing gown with his right hand and looked into the large, rather beery-looking face of PC Braithwaite.

'Good evening Sergeant,' a tactical promotion would, Taylor thought, be beneficial, 'I trust I find you well.'

PC Braithwaite blinked a few times as he took in the strange sight of a twelve year old boy in dressing gown and pyjamas who gave the impression of having just crawled out from the river.

Chapter 10

Mr Pine Explains

For the first ten minutes after Taylor, Ben and Sarah left, Mr Pine sat sipping the sherry and trying not to think about what had just happened. But even alcohol could not for ever prevent his mind from turning to his disastrous failure to impose anything that might be called authority on the boys.

It was not just the events of that evening. For weeks – no – for months - he had been doing his best not to face up to the truth that he was simply not cut out to be a school master. When he had first arrived at Portland Court he had been full of optimism. Then, after a matter of days, it had begun to dawn on him that he might not be a natural teacher. It was only in his second lesson that the boys had got the better of him.

It had started without his having any idea what they were up to. He grimaced as he remembered the humiliation. How on earth could he have allowed it to happen? Surely, he thought, any other master would have cottoned on immediately. Why had he gone marching on into the trap they had set for him?

He took another gulp of sherry as he tried to banish the memory of the catastrophe from his mind.

But it didn't work, not even for a moment.

The glass was still touching his lips as the horrid picture of what had happened in the very next lesson came to his mind. How could Latin declension end up with all ten boys doing handstands on their desks?

He shuddered and staggered to his feet. Another slug of Amontillado might do the trick.

His hand, rather shakily, had just made contact with the neck of the bottle when the door opened. He turned to see who had arrived, almost terrified that it might be another boy, but, thank the Lord, it wasn't.

His relief at seeing the headmaster only lasted a second or two. Despite his state of inebriation, his mind seemed to clear, that is to say that it cleared enough for him to grasp the fact that Mr Spencer could well be perturbed to discover that the duty master, the Under Matron and ten of the boys had set off, late at night, in search of ....

What were they in search of?

That made it worse. How could he explain the bizarre events he had witnessed without actually having any understanding of what they had been?

Sometimes, when a chap has had just that little bit too much to drink, he feels it necessary to tackle a problem head on, even though it is not a problem that requires tackling at all. That is what happened to Mr Pine. If he had been entirely sober, he would have remained silent. Mr Spencer would have gone to bed, after his own glass of sherry, quite ignorant of what had been going on in his school while he had been at the pub. But Mr Pine suddenly felt it incumbent on him to tell all. The difficulty was that he had hardly any idea what "all" might be.

'Ah, headmaster,' he started, and then couldn't quite think how to go on.

'That would be very kind', said Mr Spencer, assuming, from the way his junior colleague was holding the bottle, that Mr Pine was suggesting a glass of sherry.

'I'm sure it was,' said poor Mr Pine, who had somehow got it into his head that the headmaster was referring to Ben's decision to allow Taylor to take a contingent of boys across the river and to set off on some other venture with Sarah in the car, 'I'm convinced they were acting out of kindness, other than Taylor of course, misguided though it may have been.'

He put the bottle down and backed away from the drinks' table.

'I meant to say, Pine,' said Mr Spencer, deciding there was little point in trying to work out what Mr Pine was talking about, 'that a glass of sherry would be welcome.'

Mr Pine was now very confused indeed.

'But I was just thinking, headmaster, that I may have had enough sherry already, especially as you may need me to go in search of Taylor and Glossop.'

Mr Spencer was not exactly thinking all that lucidly himself. He had stayed in the pub for another three rounds after Mr Pine had left and the drinks had not had the result of making his thought processes all that clear. The suggestion that Mr Pine might have to go in search of Taylor and Ben did not register at all.

'I didn't mean you should have some sherry, Pine, I meant I might have a drop.'

'Oh, very sensible, headmaster,' said Mr Pine, lurching back to the table, 'In these times of crisis a glass of sherry can do wonders.'

It was the word "crisis" that got home.

'What do you mean, Pine? What crisis?' Mr Spencer had a sudden fear that the suppliers of Kennedy's Latin Primer might, finally, have decided to send in the bailiffs.

'I only meant Taylor and Glossop and the Watson girl, and the canoes, and the river, and all that', said Mr Pine, managing at the same time to spill half of what was left in the sherry bottle onto the floor.

At least it wasn't the bailiffs.

'Oh really, Pine,' said Mr Spencer in exasperation, 'let me pour the drink.'

Mr Pine, as ever terrified of irritating the headmaster, was determined to do the honours. Sadly, however, he only succeeded in knocking the bottle to the floor and emptying its entire contents.

It was as Mr Spencer, sighing heavily, went to the cupboard to find a second bottle, that the other masters made their entrance. Mr Spencer turned towards them and explained what had happened.

'Pine is somewhat agitated and has dropped the bottle. He is concerned that ... '

The headmaster suddenly realised he had no idea what it was that had concerned Mr Pine. As soon as it had become evident it was not the bailiffs, Mr Spencer had decided there was nothing to worry about, and yet it was obvious that Mr Pine was worried about something.

'You'd better explain the problem in your own words, Pine,' said Mr Spencer as he took a new bottle from the cupboard.

Mr Pine looked from one master to the next and wished he had succeeded in filling his own glass before this ordeal had begun.

The trouble was that he now seemed to have even less of an idea than he had had earlier of what it was he had to say, but he knew he had to explain. He fell back into the sofa and embarked on his story.

'Well, it all started when I saw Taylor and the other boy, a new boy he must be, didn't know him you see .... ' The hiccough didn't help, but he went on. ' .... So I was going to cane them, obviously ... ' He looked at his audience, hoping for approval of his intention to impose his authority but the other masters seemed only to be interested in what the headmaster was doing with the sherry bottle He hiccoughed again and continued. 'That was when Glossop turned up. Really,' Mr Pine was still cross with Ben, 'I think it was a bit much of him. It's frightfully difficult to do this job if one is constantly undermined. He ought to know better. Those boys needed to be punished but Glossop stopped it. Whatever may have happened to the Watson girl, he should have backed me up. Well, that's what I think.'

Mr Pine's story appeared to have come to an end. He certainly showed no sign of having anything else to add, mainly because he wasn't sure what it was he was trying to explain. It was only Mr Spencer, whose glass was now charged (and who knew about the threat to Sam), whose ears pricked up at the reference to something having "happened to the Watson girl".

'What do you mean, Pine?' exclaimed the headmaster, 'What's happened to Watson?'

'Nothing, I imagine,' said Mr Pine, 'it was just a typical schoolboy's ruse to get out of a punishment.' He sank back in the sofa and closed his eyes.

But Mr Spencer's interest was now aroused. He walked towards Mr Pine and kicked the master's right shin.

'Which schoolboy came up with the ruse?'

Mr Pine winced in pain and opened his eyes. For a second he thought of giving in his notice and leaving Portland Court forever. But, despite the beer and sherry, something told him it would be foolish to burn his boats.

'Taylor, of course,' he grunted, 'the boy who's behind all the trouble in this school.'

Mr Spencer sighed heavily. He was not a stupid man, though he might, at that moment, have been a little intoxicated. He was perfectly well aware of the role Taylor played in keeping Portland Court afloat. What is more, he knew all that Taylor had done to ensure Mr Pine's lessons were no longer the farces they had been at the beginning.

'Oh, really, Pine,' the headmaster was exasperated, 'don't talk nonsense. Taylor is entirely trustworthy. Tell us immediately what did he say happened to Watson?'

Mr Pine was beginning to think the whole world was against him. It had been bad enough when Ben had prevented him from caning Taylor, but now the headmaster himself was backing the boy. He was unable to contain his annoyance.

'I really don't understand, headmaster .... ' he decided to get up from the sofa in order make his point more forcefully, ' .... why you should all .... ' He fell to the floor for the second time that evening. However he had started and he was determined to finish. He picked himself up, brushed himself down, and continued, 'I can't imagine why you all think that boy is so wonderful. He came up with a cock and bull story this evening, just to avoid a well deserved beating. This school is doomed while you refuse to expel Taylor.'

Mr Rice and Mr Green, who had now, like Mr Spencer, managed to acquire glasses full of sherry and were therefore able to concentrate, in a way, on what was being said, looked at each other in astonishment. Only half an hour ago they had been discussing the vexed question of whether Portland Court would survive Taylor's departure for public school. The idea that Taylor might be removed even before his common entrance examination was not one they had ever considered.

But it was Mr Spencer who spoke first. 'Pine, I require you to answer the question. What did Taylor say about Watson?'

Mr Pine looked in turn at each of his colleagues. Their expressions did not suggest to him that he had any allies in the room. He descended, once again, to the sofa. 'It was nonsense, headmaster,' he said as he regained the safety of his seat. 'He told me, in order, I remind you, to get out of a thrashing, that Watson had been kidnapped and, which is much worse, young Glossop was taken in. That's why the boys have gone off in canoes and Glossop has taken the car.'

* * *

As Mr Spencer and the other masters were attempting to follow Mr Pine's confused story, Taylor was desperately trying to think of the best way of getting rid of PC Braithwaite.

'Perhaps, my lad,' the constable said, 'you would care to explain to me what you are doing?'

Taylor's mind raced. His task was not easy. If Matron had not been crouching a few feet away, quite likely to shift her position very noisily at any second, he would have been confident of his ability to send the policeman on his way, but he didn't have that luxury. He had to produce an almost instant result, and he had to do it despite the combined facts that it was very late at night, that he was only twelve years old and that he was standing by a river bank in his pyjamas and dressing gown.

'Were you not told, Sergeant .... ?' He had toyed with the idea of elevating the constable to the rank of Inspector but had concluded that that might be going too far. ' .... We were told all local police stations had been alerted.'

As he said it, Taylor could see he had got it right. He was fortunate, though he had no notion of this, that PC Braithwaite had spent a large part of the day complaining that his superiors felt it quite unnecessary to keep him in touch with divisional police investigations.

Taylor was also helped by PC Braithwaite's unusually low IQ. Instead of realising that the child who was addressing him was trying to lead him up the garden path, his immediate thought was that, yet again, he had not been informed of some secret operation. And his next thought was that it would be a very bad thing if this boy were to run away with the impression he didn't know what was happening.

'Ah,' he said after a pause for thought, 'yes, I was expecting to run into you.'

Taylor couldn't believe his luck. He thought for a second and then rammed home his advantage.

'Excellent, Officer, but we must continue as planned. You must return to the station and await further instructions.' In a moment he had understood the man with whom he was dealing. He knew he could go even further. 'The Chief Constable,' he said with a knowing nod, 'will hear of your contribution.'

PC Braithwaite glowed with pride. He may not have been told of this particular operation but, when it was successful (and he would make sure it was successful by doing as the boy said), the Chief Constable would be told of the vital part he had played.

'And, young man,' said the constable solemnly, 'I shall inform the Chief Constable of your own valuable assistance as well.'

Just as the policeman seemed to be about to set off on his bicycle, Matron moved. Taylor's heart sank.

There could be no other explanation for the sound. It wasn't just a twig breaking, it sounded like a whole forest being felled. Taylor reacted instantly.

'Quick, Sergeant,' he barked the order, 'it sounds as though they're near. Back to the station.'

Cecil Braithwaite looked doubtful, but only for a second. Stupid he might be, but he was bright enough to grasp that his confident assertion that he had been expecting to see the boy made it rather difficult to start casting doubt on what was happening.

'Right you are, my lad,' he said as he mounted his squeaky bicycle again, 'and good luck.'

Taylor let out a long but silent sigh of relief as he watched the constable ride off. He was particularly glad he had not been asked for any details of the secret operation on which he was engaged. My own guess, however, is that he would have had little difficulty in providing those details.

* * *

Back at Portland Court, Mr Spencer acted decisively. He knew he was drunk. He knew the other masters were drunk. He knew the best hope lay with Taylor. But he also knew Portland Court would not survive the loss of Sam. It was time for action.

'Pine,' he commanded, 'you will stay here, in charge of the other boys. The rest of you must come with me. We will use canoes.'

Chapter 11

The Chase is On

As PC Braithwaite's squeaking bicycle wobbled round the corner at the end of the road, Taylor breathed easily again. He turned back to the river bank. 'OK, lads, and Matron, you can come out now.'

The ten boys scrambled up the bank. Matron, whose physique wasn't built for such things, took a little longer, and a helping hand from Taylor, to get to the road, but she made it eventually.

'Right,' she puffed as she joined Taylor and his troops, 'into action. Taylor, lead me to the villains. The rest of you stay here. There's no need for you to take any risks.'

'I'm afraid it's not as simple as that, Matron,' Taylor sighed again as he contemplated the complications Matron would cause, 'we don't know where they are. That is to say, we know they are on their way to this village, but we don't know the address they will go to.'

'Goodness me, do you mean to say you've made me take that treacherous voyage across the river for no purpose at all? What were you thinking of?'

Perhaps she was still affected by the drug. Taylor thought he'd better be charitable.

'Actually, Matron, no one made you come over here but that's not the point. What we have to do now is spread out and make sure at least one of us sees where their car goes. Then we'll make our plans.'

Matron was silent for a moment as she took this in. 'But,' she still seemed unsure, 'how will we know which their car is?'

'Fortunately,' Taylor signalled for Tim to step forward, 'Crane here knows exactly what type of car they have.'

Matron peered at the only properly dressed boy and clapped a hand to her mouth to muffle her gasp.

'But that's Marrow's son.' she exclaimed. 'We have a traitor in our midst. Seize him boys,' and she made to grab him.

Taylor was too quick for her. He jumped in front of Tim to ward off the attack.

'No, Matron, he's not Marrow's son. He's a thoroughly decent boy from the village who's given us a massive amount of help.'

'Really, Taylor, how can you be so foolish? For goodness sake, you showed him round the school yourself.'

The complications were going to be worse than he had thought.

'I'm sorry, Matron,' there was that steeliness in his voice again, the tone he had used in her bedroom, 'we haven't got time for this. I will explain it all later. Now,' he turned away from Matron and addressed the boys, 'the car's likely to come on the main road, from the Barston direction, so we need most of you strung out along there. Crane, you take half a dozen of the lads and place them at hundred yard intervals all along the road. If you see the car, watch where it goes and come back to report to me.'

Tim quickly selected his team as a thoroughly perplexed Matron watched. Then he led them off to the Barston Road.

'Barker, you take the rest and cover the other two roads into the village. Same rules apply - if you see the car, keep it in sight, check where it goes and come back here.'

The other four boys set off, leaving Taylor alone with Matron, who now recovered her voice.

'Taylor, I recognise I haven't covered myself in glory tonight, but I do think you have some explaining to do. You can start by telling me why you keep addressing that Marrow boy as Crane.'

'It's quite a long story Matron, but I reckon we've got time.'

* * *

There was no warning. At one moment the car was cruising along comfortably. At the next, all power seemed to have disappeared.

The engine was still running but it was not turning the wheels. They drew slowly to a halt.

They were on a narrow part of the Barston Road, still about ten miles from Marlbury. There were trees on both sides of the road overhanging it and cutting out the moonlight. They hadn't seen another car for the last ten minutes. Ben raised his hands and brought them down forcibly on the steering wheel.

'Oh no. That's all we need.' He turned to Sam's father. 'I'm so sorry, sir. I just don't know what's happened.'

'Fan belt, I should think,' Mr Watson was opening the door. He turned to Sarah. 'You don't happen to be wearing stockings do you?'

She understood immediately. 'Yes, hang on. I'll take one off.'

Ben was no mechanic. His grasp of the workings of the internal combustion engine was pretty weak but even he now remembered hearing how a woman's stocking could be used to fashion a temporary fan belt.

A moment later Sarah was handing a nylon stocking to Mr Watson. 'Will that do?'

'Just the thing,' he walked round to the front of the car and lifted the bonnet. Then he fished a small torch out of his pocket and shone it into the engine.

'As I thought,' he pulled out a broken fan belt and passed it to

Ben, 'this won't take a moment.' He doubled up the stocking and leant back inside the bonnet.

As he did so, the headlights of what was clearly a large car coming up behind them shone straight at him. It was going at quite a speed but the driver must have seen them in time. He slowed to a halt beside the battered Morris Minor Traveller.

'Need any help, guv?' the driver was leaning across the passenger seat towards the open window.

'No, it's all right thanks,' but then Mr Watson made out the features of the man. 'Goodness, Griffiths, fancy seeing you here.'

'Is that you, Mr Watson?' the man opened his door and stepped out.

'It is. What brings you to this neck of the woods, Griffiths?'

'I'm to go and meet Sir George, sir, at Marlbury. Don't know what's up. Just had this call. He said he needed me urgently. I'd offer you a lift, but I daren't go further than Marlbury. Seems I'm wanted in a hurry.'

Mr Watson thought for a moment and appeared to make up his mind.

'Actually, we're going to Marlbury ourselves. You know, it really would be uncommonly kind of you to give me a lift there. With any luck I've fixed the problem here but it might go wrong again. Would you mind it if I jumped in with you and you let my friends follow in their car?'

'No problem, sir. Here, I'll open the door for you.'

'Thank you so much. I just need to get something from inside the car. Won't be a second.'

Mr Watson went round to the side of the Morris where Ben and Sarah were standing. As he leant inside, pretending to get something out, he whispered to them.

'I think we're onto something. Can't explain now, but follow Sir George's car.'

* * *

Taylor had finished the story. Matron's eyes were bulging in amazement. She wasn't sure she had followed it all but it was definitely an extraordinary tale.

'Goodness, Taylor. Is it really true?

'Completely, Matron.' He turned towards the river bank. 'What on earth is that row?'

A great deal of splashing could be heard from a few feet below him. He scrambled down the bank and peered towards the noise. It didn't take him long to work out what it was. He could hear a voice he knew all too well.

'Do watch what you're doing with that paddle, Green. You nearly knocked me out.'

'Sorry, headmaster, but it's awfully dark. Do you think we've got to the right place?'

'Well, we've got to Marlbury and I can't imagine where else Taylor and the other boys were heading.'

Taylor climbed back up. 'What have I done to deserve this? It looks like the whole of the masters' common room has turned up. Matron, will you help me?'

The time for doubting Taylor had long passed. 'Of course I will. What do you want me to do?'

Taylor's mind was racing. He had to get the headmaster and the others out of the way quickly. He had an idea.

'OK, Matron, here's the plan. Do you know where the Nag's Head is?'

There were very few pubs and hotels in the district with which Matron was not familiar.

'Yes, just up the road from here.'

'Good. I want you to take Mr Spencer and the others there. With any luck the landlord will still be up. Talk him into letting them take a room or two. He'll welcome the business, especially if they say they'll buy some drinks in the bar. Tell them it's going to be our headquarters and say I'll join them later.'

Matron frowned. 'But what about me? I've got to be there when you find Marrow.'

'Don't worry, Matron, I'll send a messenger to get you. But you must see, we can't have that lot getting in the way and mucking everything up. They're probably not as sober as you.'

As he spoke, the headmaster and Mr Green were making their way, much too noisily, up the river bank.

'Ah, splendid,' bellowed Mr Spencer as he spotted Taylor, 'we've come to the right place. 'Oh, Matron, what are you doing here?'

'Helping Taylor, headmaster.'

'Jolly good show,' his voice was carrying half way across the village.

'Sorry to sound rude, sir,' Taylor was looking up and down the road, terrified that Marrow's car might appear at any moment, 'but do you think you could keep your voice down?'

Mr Spencer made as though to reprimand the boy, but thought better of it.

'Quite right, Taylor,' he whispered, 'can't be giving our whereabouts away. This is your show, boy, not ours. Look on us as your eager troops, ready to obey your every command.'

Taylor glanced down to see yet more bedraggled and wet masters clambering up to the road. His heart sank at the sight. He turned back to the headmaster.

'That's very kind of you, sir. What would be very helpful, if I might suggest it, would be if you and the other masters took charge of our headquarters. Matron will take you there. It'll be enormously useful to have some responsible adults in control of things.'

'Just say the word, Taylor, and we'll do your bidding. Righty ho, Matron, where's the headquarters?'

'The Nag's head, headmaster, just follow me.'

Mr Green, who had been looking rather fed up after his arduous river crossing, seemed to perk up considerably at the news that they were to be based in a pub. His fellow masters were equally cheered by the announcement as, one by one, they fought their way up to the road and were told of their destination.

Taylor, as he watched the gaggle of obviously intoxicated masters swaying their way up the road, led by a very large and self-important Matron, prayed the Nag's Head landlord would let them in.

* * *

'Not long now, young lady,' Bert Jones's chuckle as he spoke sounded thoroughly evil and malevolent, ‘time for the blindfold.’

Sam had worked out they were heading in the direction of Marlbury. She had been determined to ensure she kept track of their route but now it seemed she was to be blindfolded. For a moment she thought of struggling, of trying to stop it being put in place, but that would be hopeless. These two thugs may not be the most intelligent men in the county but they were certainly strong. Meekly she submitted as the man she knew as Marrow tied the dirty rag around her head.

But she wouldn’t give up her attempt to memorise the route. She had read stories about how people worked out where they were being taken while blindfolded. She knew what to do. She would count slowly until the first turning. Then start counting again until the next, and so on. With any luck she would be able to guide the police to wherever they were going, once she had escaped.

* * *

Tim was the first to spot the car. He couldn’t tell, as its headlights appeared in the distance, whether it was the Rover but, as it got closer, he became sure it was. As soon as it was past him he frantically waved a white handkerchief, a pre-arranged sign, at

Parsons, the boy further down the road.

Parsons saw. He, too, waited for it to pass, then he waved the white stick he had found in the road at Mitchell Major. The car was going straight on. It didn't turn down Coronation Road but it was slowing.

Mitchell Major hoped his slipper was a light enough colour to be seen by Perkins. It was. He could make out the boy signalling ahead.

The four of them, Tim, Parsons, Mitchell Major and Perkins, were now running after the car. It slowed almost to a halt and turned left down Church Lane. Thank goodness. Barker's boys were down there.

Perkins got to the junction first. The car must have been close to Barker's position. Perkins had removed his pyjama top. He waved it at where he hoped Barker was. He was rewarded by the sight of the head boy starting his sprint.

The car slowed again and turned right. Barker knew it was a cul de sac. They must be almost there. But there were no boys down that road. He ran faster, desperate to get to the turning in time to see which drive the car turned into. He knew all the houses had long drives. If he didn't see which one the car went for it could take an age to track it down.

He was too late. As he got to the turning, he could see no

vehicles ahead. It could have gone into any of twenty drives. It was tempting to start the search straight away but he knew that would be wrong. Taylor would have to be told. All the boys would be needed.

Perkins, breathing heavily, caught up with Barker.

'Did you see where it went?'

'No, worse luck. Look, we'd better round up all the lads. You go and tell Taylor. I'll wait here.'

* * *

Matron was hammering heavily on the locked door of the Nag's Head. There was one upstairs light on but the ground floor was in darkness. Eventually, a light appeared in the hallway and a voice could be heard from inside.

'All right, all right, I'm coming.'

Matron stopped her knocking and composed herself for the negotiations. She had already told the masters to stand back so the publican wouldn't immediately see them. The sight, she was sure, would be bound to lead him to a firm resolution not to admit them to his inn.

The door opened slightly. It was on a chain. Jim Cartwright was not taking any chances.

'What is it?' He was wearing a dressing gown, that much she could see.

'Good evening, Inn Keeper,' she hoped she sounded calm and thoroughly respectable. 'We wondered whether you might have some rooms for the night. Our car's broken down and we have nowhere to stay.'

He peered out at the formidably large woman, hesitated for a second and thought of how much he could charge.

'How many are you?'

'Six.'

'Goodness me, I ain't got six rooms in the whole place.'

'Two or three will be plenty. We don't mind doubling up.'

'Well, I suppose we could do something for you. Mind you, there's only bread and cheese to eat, but I could open the bar for you if you'd like.'

Matron was in two minds about the bar. The walk from the river had been enough to make it abundantly clear to her that all the masters had already had more than an aperitif, but her own mouth was feeling somewhat dry, probably something to do with Marrow's drug. And, of course, Taylor wanted them all kept out of the way.

'That would be splendid. We'll be no trouble.'

Mr Cartwright released the chain and pulled the door wide.

As he did so, Mr Spencer lurched forward. For a second, the publican thought of slamming the door shut again until he recognised the swaying figure.

'Why, if it isn't Mr Spencer. A bit the worse for wear are we, sir?'

'Just tired,' the headmaster affected a yawn, 'it's been a long night.'

'I expect so, sir, probably in need of a tincture or two, I dare say.' It might have been nice to go to bed but there were very few publicans in the county who weren't aware that the headmaster of Portland Court and his staff could do wonders for the bar takings.

'Well, maybe a little drop wouldn't come amiss.'

Mr Cartwright ushered the schoolmasters and Matron in.

* * *

Perkins hadn't run so much for ages. He was panting furiously as he reached Taylor.

'They're here.'

'Right, where?'

Perkins had to get his breath back but he managed to answer. 'Spilsbury Lane, but we don't know which house.'

'Blast.' Taylor thought for a moment. 'Very well, round up all the lads. Get them to the top of Spilsbury Lane. We'll make a plan when we're all there.'

* * *

Sam had counted to a hundred and fifty before the car turned to the left. Then another seventy before it turned to the right. Now it was on gravel, probably a drive to a house. It was a long one. She counted to twenty. The car stopped.

'Blindfold stays on till we're inside.' Marrow, or Jones, pulled her arm. She followed him out of the car. 'Knock on the door, Jeff. They're expecting us.'

Jeff Porter, or "Mr Turnip", lifted the knocker and brought it down once. In an instant the door opened.

'Get her upstairs, men.' Sam thought she knew the voice, but she couldn't place it.

'Very well, Sir ... '

'Never use my name,' the man interrupted instantly. 'Come on, get a move on.'

* * *

‘Where do you want in Marlbury, sir?’ Griffiths was keeping a careful watch in the rear view mirror to make sure Ben and Sarah remained in sight.

‘Just drop me where you’re going.’ Mr Watson knew this bit could be difficult. ‘It sounds as though you’re in a fearful hurry. My friends can take me on.’

‘It’ll be no trouble, sir. Just give me the address and I’ll take you there.’

‘Do you know, odd though it must seem, I’m not sure of the address. The others know it. They’ll find it, don’t worry.’

‘Well, if you’re sure, sir. Shouldn’t be long now.’

* * *

‘What do you think he meant by saying we were onto something?’ Ben couldn’t help glancing down at Sarah’s stockingless right leg as he spoke.

‘I’ve no idea but he certainly seemed to know what he was doing. And I wonder who Sir George is?’

‘Probably some sort of business associate, I expect, but it’s a bit of a coincidence that he’s in Marlbury.’

* * *

'Matron, ladies first, what will you have?'

Mr Spencer felt reassured to be back in a bar. Jim Cartwright, still in his dressing gown, was waiting to serve the drinks.

'Well, I shouldn't really, headmaster, not with so much ahead of us, but maybe just a very small double gin and tonic.'

'Very wise, Matron. And, gentlemen,' he turned to the other masters, 'a little cognac perhaps?'

They nodded their approval of this suggestion.

'I tell you what, my man .... ' he was smarting a little at the publican's earlier cheekiness and was now determined to show his superiority. "My man" should do the trick. ' .... why don't you pop off to bed. We'll look after ourselves. Just leave a bottle of cognac on the bar.' He patted his pockets. 'You can send me the bill to Portland Court.'

Mr Cartwright's complexion paled.

'If you don't mind, sir, I prefer cash up front, so to speak.'

'Really?' Mr Spencer turned to the others, 'this is dashed awkward but I don't seem to have any money on me.'

They all sighed as one but knew their duty. Pockets were emptied and between them they produced 15s/4d.

'Will that do, barman?' Mr Spencer handed over the collection of coins.

'Admirably, sir, I'll leave this bottle of brandy and maybe a little gin as well, for the lady. Shall I show you the way to your rooms now?'

'No,' Mr Spencer was well aware, and he was sure Cartwright was as well, that the rooms were no more than a way round the licensing laws, 'I'm sure we'll find our way.'

'Very well, sir, I'll turn in now, but, of course, if you use the rooms there will be a further charge.' That, he was sure, would be enough to make sure no sheets would have to be changed in the morning.

Once the drinks were poured, the strange group settled down by the still glowing fire.

'Now, Matron,' Mr Spencer took a sip from his glass, 'you'd better fill us in. Pine wasn't exactly clear on what's been going on.'

* * *

'Are we all here?' Taylor counted the boys gathered round him. 'Good, now let's make our plan.'

None of his listeners felt it likely that the plan would be made by anyone other than Taylor but neither did any feel any resentment. This was a crisis and, in a crisis, there was only one boy to whom one should turn.

'The first thing is to do a recce of all the houses. We need to know which ones have lights on. Any in darkness can probably be excluded. Once we've narrowed the field, we'll meet here again and decide the next stage.'

They heard the sound of a car approaching.

'Quick,' Taylor pointed, 'behind that hedge.'

It wasn't just one car. There were two. And the second one, they could all see as it turned the corner, was the school Morris Minor Traveller. The first was a very large black limousine.

The two cars drove down Spilsbury Lane in what appeared to be convoy. The first one slowed and came to a halt just by the driveway to the third house on the right. The second one stopped behind it.

Taylor peered out from behind the hedge. The passenger door of the limousine opened. A man got out. Taylor could only make out the shape but then the cloud masking the moon moved away and he could see as though it were daylight.

The man was Mr Watson, Sam's father.

Chapter 12

Can They Save Her?

PC Braithwaite was deeply troubled, and the more he thought about the strange boy by the river bank, the more troubled he became. Why would divisional headquarters be using a boy that age, and in dressing gown and slippers, for some top secret operation in the middle of the night? Had he been tricked? Was the boy up to no good? What should he do? He could always ring headquarters and ask them what was going on, but suppose they knew nothing about it. What would they think when he told them he'd believed the boy? No, he couldn't risk that.

Perhaps he should go back to the boy. But what if it was all true? What would they make of him at headquarters if he ruined the operation by doing what the boy said he must not do? Suppose his arrival alerted the villains, whoever they may be, to the fact that their plot, whatever it may be, was about to be foiled? No, he couldn't go back.

He would have a cup of tea. That was the answer.

He put his uniform jacket on the back of the chair behind the desk and went through to the kitchen.

It was then that the telephone rang.

PC Braithwaite didn't like the telephone. Too often its bell heralded bad news. Too often it was Sergeant Phillips finding fault. But it had to be answered, he knew that. Tempting though it was to let it ring, failing to answer it could lead to serious trouble. He took a deep breath and went back to the front room.

For a moment or two he stood over the desk staring at the telephone, then, with an audible sigh, he leant down and picked up the receiver.

'Marlbury Police House, PC Braithwaite speaking.'

'Thank goodness you're there, Officer.' He recognised the voice at once. Miss Potter, a village busybody if ever there was one.

'Good evening, Miss Potter. What seems to be the trouble?'

'I wish I knew, Officer. There's strange things going on in the village.'

Had she seen the boy as well? What was he supposed to say if she had? PC Braithwaite dreaded what was coming.

'What sort of things, Miss Potter?'

'Sinister things, Officer. Sinister things.'

'Could you be a little more explicit, Miss Potter?' He was rather pleased with that. It made him sound educated.

‘I’m not sure where to begin.’ She paused, he assumed to gather her thoughts, and continued, in a rush. ‘To start with, there are small boys all over the place, in their night clothes. Probably some jape but they should be home in bed. More importantly, from your point of view, there are some drunken men, and a large woman, illicitly drinking in the Nag’s Head.’

This was safer territory. ‘Oh dear, Miss Potter. It’s well past closing time. How do you know they’re not residents?’

‘Well, it’s obvious. I saw them from my front window. They had no suitcases, they were swaying as they walked, and when they went in they went straight to the bar. I saw the light come on.’

‘This is bad, Miss Potter. Tell me, did they seem the rough sort?’ PC Braithwaite did not relish the thought of drunkards resisting arrest.

‘You can never tell with people who’ve taken drink but I suppose they didn’t look all that rough. In fact some of them were quite elderly. But we can’t have all night drinking in Marlbury. It must be stopped.’

‘Very public spirited of you, Miss Potter. I will be along in a few minutes.’

‘Good. And I’ll keep an eye on things from my window until you get here.’

Of that, PC Braithwaite was sure.

He'd have liked that cup of tea but he knew his duty, and this might be the answer to his worries. If he could tell headquarters he was sorting out some after hours drinking while whatever else was going on in the village, he might just escape censure. After all, he couldn't be in two places at the same time.

* * *

Taylor watched as the large black car turned into the driveway of the house and Mr Watson walked back to the school Morris. The Gusset Twanger was opening his door and climbing out. Miss Wilton was getting out of the other side.

As soon as the limousine was out of sight, Taylor emerged from behind the hedge and crossed over to speak to the new arrivals.

'Aha,' this was Mr Watson, 'I see I was right. Well done, Taylor. It is Taylor, isn't it?'

'Yes, sir. We're all here.' He let out a quiet whistle and boys appeared in the road as if from nowhere.

'Excellent,' Mr Watson beamed his approval, 'so what's your plan, Taylor?'

'Well, sir, we know that Watson's been taken to a house in this road but we don't know which.'

'Goodness, I'm ahead of the famous Taylor,' Mr Watson's smile made it clear he wasn't being sarcastic. 'By chance, I can tell you which house.' He turned and pointed to the driveway down which the black car had driven. 'It's that one.'

'Golly, sir,' Taylor was impressed, 'how do you know that?'

'A stroke of luck. I've had my suspicions for some time about who's behind this plot. There's a man who's been trying to take over one of my companies. He has failed miserably to date. But, if I have to raise a large sum to pay a ransom demand, I would probably have to accept his offer. That car was being driven by his chauffeur. The coincidence, I think you will agree, is rather startling.'

'But you were in the car, sir,' Taylor was annoyed with himself for not having grasped the whole story immediately. 'Why would this man's chauffeur drive you to the house where Watson's being held?'

'He has no idea that that is what he's done. In fact, I am convinced he knows nothing about this at all. He is simply responding to his master's instruction to come here. Entirely fortuitously he came to our aid when Mr Glossop's car broke down and he offered me a lift to Marlbury. But there will be time for explanations later. What do you think we should do, Taylor?'

Taylor was quite used to masters deferring to him but he was surprised that Sam's father, who didn't know him at all, should now be doing so.

'Well, sir, don't you want to take over now?'

'Certainly not. Sam, perhaps I should call her "Watson", has told me all about you, Taylor. I have complete faith in you. So, what's the plan?'

Taylor hoped Mr Watson's faith was justified but there was no time to worry about that. 'OK, sir, first, we do have one or two small problems. I gave my word to Matron that I would send a messenger for her once we were about to start.'

'Matron?' Sarah was obviously dumbfounded, 'Is she here?'

'Yes, ma'am. She's in the Nag's Head.'

'But, I don't understand,' it was Ben's turn to be astounded, 'how did she get here?'

'By canoe sir.'

'Matron, in a canoe? Is this a dream, Taylor?'

He could understand Sarah's astonishment. 'I'll explain later, ma'am, if that's all right. But the thing is that I did give my word. So we've got no choice really. Actually, though, she's not in a bad way, if you know what I mean, at least she wasn't when she went to the Nag's Head.'

'And what,' Mr Watson asked, 'are the other problems?'

'Mr Spencer and all the other masters, except Mr Pine.'

Ben's eyes were wide with incredulity. 'You're not going to tell us they're here as well?'

'I'm afraid so, sir. I think Mr Pine must have told them. It's frightfully decent of them to have come but, well, I think they may be a little tired, or something like that.'

Despite everything, Mr Watson grinned. 'And these learned gentlemen are also in the Nag's Head?'

'Exactly, sir. So we have to get Matron out without them following. But I've thought about that. Crane can go over there now. He's really brilliant, sir. He'll carry it off. He can tell Mr Spencer and the others they're needed at headquarters - that's what we're calling the Nag's Head. With any luck they will have made themselves comfortable and not be all that keen to leave.'

'Right,' Mr Watson's grin had gone, 'and what do we do when Matron gets here'

* * *

'You can take the blindfold off now.'

Sam had stumbled up two flights of stairs and was being pushed by Bert Jones into a small room with a bare electric light bulb and shuttered windows. As she pulled the blindfold from her head she turned to see the door closing behind her. It was a padded door. Obviously soundproofing. She went over to the window. The shutters were fixed firmly in place; she couldn't prise them open. She went back to the door and tried the handle. It was no good, the lock was clearly new and strong.

She felt a stinging in her eyes. There were tears. She knew she mustn't give in. She blinked furiously and sat on the cold floor, determined to think of a plan.

* * *

PC Braithwaite's bicycle was wobbling its way towards the Nag's Head. He'd worked out what he would do. He would peer through the bar window to check that the men, and the large woman, didn't look too rough. If they didn't, he would press on and make some arrests. If they did, well, then he would need to think again.

As he turned the corner into the High Street, he suddenly applied the brakes.

There was a boy at the front door to the Nag's Head. Not, he didn't know why this was a relief, a boy in dressing gown and slippers, but definitely a boy.

This was getting even more complicated. Was this infestation of boys somehow connected with the illicit drinking? Was the divisional operation something to do with out of hours drinking? Should he go on or would it be wiser to wait and watch?

There was only one answer. He dismounted and crept to the side of the road, in the shadows.

The boy was knocking on the door. It opened but it wasn't Cartwright who opened it, PC Braithwaite could see that. It was a large woman, a mountain of a woman. She and the boy spoke for a few seconds. Then, with a quick look back, the woman came out and pulled the door shut behind her. She and the boy crossed the road together, walking quickly. They didn't see him as they passed.

Now what? He looked up and down the street. No one else seemed to be around. There was no noise of depravity coming from the pub. He could just go home to the police house. He could have that cup of tea, but then he saw Miss Potter's house. More to the point, he saw her net curtain move. He would have to go on. She would be straight onto the telephone to headquarters if he didn't.

* * *

'Where did Matron go?' Mr Green was filling the glasses.

'I've no idea,' Mr Spencer's eyelids were drooping, 'but I'm sure she'll be back soon. Extraordinary story, wasn't it?'

'Indeed, headmaster.' Mr Rice also felt the evening's exertions catching up with him. 'I wonder what Taylor will want us to do.'

'He'll have everything under control,' Mr Spencer nodded as he spoke, as if to confirm the wisdom of his words, 'but it's quite right we're here, in the midst of the action, so to speak. It's just like Dunkirk all over again. Goodness, what we go through for our boys, and girl, of course.'

'Quite so, headmaster,' Mr Green was lowering himself back into the armchair. 'I confess I never thought I would become a sort of James Bond when I went into prep' school teaching.'

The masters fell into a companionable silence.

'What on earth is that?' Mr Spencer's eyes had closed but they were now wide open again.

The loud knocking was accompanied by speech. 'Open up in the name of the law.'

It came from the street.

Mr Spencer pulled himself to his feet. 'Of course, Taylor's sent the constabulary to get us to come and help. I'll let them in.'

He stumbled slightly as he walked out to the hall but he soon recovered his balance. By the time he opened the front door, he was sure he was entirely presentable.

'Ah, splendid, Officer. What does Taylor require?'

PC Braithwaite's mouth opened and shut three times but he found his voice. 'Are you aware of the licensing laws in this country, sir?'

'Is this some sort of code, Constable? Come on, out with it, what does Taylor wish us to do?'

PC Braithwaite decided that a more direct approach was required. 'I must require you to come with me, sir.'

'Getting to the point at last. I'll just get the others.'

PC Braithwaite couldn't claim to understand exactly what was happening but at least it appeared they were going to come quietly. He waited as the elderly man went back into the bar and re-emerged, followed by several other middle-aged-to-elderly men in tweed jackets.

'Lead on, officer. Take us to Taylor.' Mr Spencer strode out.

'Hang on, headmaster,' Mr Green seemed to be agitated. 'What about Matron. Where is she?'

'Good point, Green,' Mr Spencer stopped and turned back towards the pub. 'Someone had better look for her.'

PC Braithwaite felt the need to impose his authority.

'No you don't, sir. No one's going back inside.'

'I am fully aware, officer,' Mr Spencer pulled his shoulders back as he spoke, 'that this is a dreadfully serious situation we face but we cannot just leave Matron. Taylor would be horrified.'

'Who is Matron?'

'*Who is Matron?*' Mr Spencer clearly thought he was dealing with an imbecile. 'Surely Taylor must have told you about Matron.'

'No-one has told me about Matron, sir.' PC Braithwaite was thoroughly confused and had the feeling he was losing control.

'I find that most odd. Never mind. Matron is central to this operation. She was here a few minutes ago but she disappeared.'

'Could she be a rather large lady, sir?'

'Ah, you have it. I knew you would have been told about her. Yes, you are correct. Matron is no midget.'

PC Braithwaite knew he shouldn't be encouraging this bizarre conversation but he was at a loss as to what else to do. 'She left a moment ago, with a boy.'

'With a boy you say, yes, that will be her. Point the way, Officer. There is no time to be lost.'

He regretted it as soon as he did it but PC Braithwaite pointed towards Spilsbury Lane.

'Well, come on, man. What are you waiting for?' Mr Spencer marched off, followed by his companions.

PC Braithwaite grabbed his bicycle and set off in pursuit of his prey.

* * *

'Do you know, Taylor,' Mr Watson had listened without interruption to the boy's plan, 'I think it might work. All we need is Matron.'

'I think I can hear her now.' Taylor turned to look down the lane. He was right. Matron was lumbering towards them with Tim at her side.

Taylor signalled to the other boys. In an instant, and without further instruction, they set off down the drive and began to fan out around the house. Taylor waited for Matron.

'I'm sorry to ask you to do this, Matron,' he sounded as though he meant it, 'but it's our best hope.'

'Whatever you ask, I will do.' Taylor was pleased to note that she had obviously not had too much to drink. 'Give me your orders, Taylor.'

* * *

'Griffiths,' Sir George had summoned the chauffeur into the drawing room, 'is the car fully fuelled?'

'Yes, sir. I filled up in Barston.'

'Good, we will leave in ten minutes.'

'You'll never believe who I met ... '

But Sir George interrupted. 'No time for gossip, Griffiths. Wait in the hall.'

'Oh, righty ho, Sir George.'

'And send Jones in. But don't go upstairs, is that understood?'

'Yes, sir.' Griffiths was perplexed. Never had he seen his employer so agitated before. Still, his was not to reason why. He went out to the hall and called upstairs.

'Bert, Sir George wants you.'

Bert Jones, also known as Mr Marrow, appeared on the first floor landing.

'Just coming. You stay down there, got that?'

It really was most peculiar.

* * *

The boys, Mr Watson, Ben and Sarah watched as Matron strode up to the front door. All knew their roles. All were holding their breath as they prayed Taylor's plan would work.

* * *

The doorbell rang. Bert was in the drawing room. There was someone else upstairs. Griffiths didn't know who it was but there was no-one else to open the door. He stepped towards it and turned the handle moments before Jones rushed out from the drawing room.

'Shut it, you fool,' Jones bellowed.

But it was too late. The door was open and a giant of a woman was standing there.

'I insist,' she said with a tone of menace in her voice, 'on seeing Mr Marrow.'

Jones couldn't see her but he knew the voice. He waved at Griffiths, signalling for him to get rid of their visitor.

Griffiths looked at Jones, then looked at the woman, then looked back at Jones.

'Get rid of her', Jones mouthed.

He turned back to the woman. 'There is no Mr Marrow here. I think you must have the wrong address.'

'I will stand no nonsense.' She didn't look as though she would. 'I know Benjamin Marrow is here and I insist on seeing him.'

She was now halfway in. Jones, terrified he would be seen, darted back into the drawing room.

'I promise you, madam, there is no Mr Marrow here.' Griffiths was doing his best, but everything was becoming very difficult.

* * *

'What the blazes is going on?' Sir George was now standing.

'I don't understand it, sir,' Jones was genuinely confused, 'it's that matron from Portland Court.'

'What is she doing here? How did she find us?'

'I don't know. She was fast asleep when I left her, drugged to the eyeballs.'

'Get Griffiths to get rid of her.'

'I don't think I can, sir. She's got her foot in the door.'

'Do you think she knows anything?'

'I wouldn't have thought so, sir. She's not that bright.'

'So, why do you think she's here?'

Jones blushed as he answered. 'I think she's rather fallen for me, sir.'

'How very odd. Well, you'll have to get rid of her yourself. No, get her upstairs. Lock her in with the girl. You'll have to send Griffiths out to the car. We can't risk him knowing any of this.'

* * *

The watchers could see Matron was halfway into the house. The chauffeur was remonstrating with her but he'd never be able to budge her.

The plan was working.

Then the chauffeur came out, past Matron, and walked to the black car. Matron took another step inside. They could just see Marrow apparently letting her in. This was too good to be true.

Yes, it was. The silence was suddenly broken. 'This way, gentlemen.' Why did Mr Spencer have to bellow?

Taylor turned and saw his headmaster, followed by several other masters and an obviously distraught police constable. They were all heading straight for the house.

But Matron saw too. She was not nearly as stupid as Jones had suggested. The plan had to be changed. Without any warning of any sort she drew her right arm back. All the boys had seen that movement before. Matron may not take much exercise but her right arm had the muscles of a prize fighter. When attached to a large leather slipper it could produce the sort of sting that made the eyes water. There was no slipper this time but her fist was clenched. Taylor was not the only one to wince in sympathy as he saw that fist swinging violently towards Mr Marrow's nose.

And they heard her words too.

'You are a cad, Marrow, and you will pay the price.'

Taylor knew they had to act immediately. He let out a loud whistle and every boy in the garden reacted instantly.

As Marrow, or whatever his name was, fell back, blood pouring from his nose, ten boys rushed in.

* * *

Sir George heard the noise and dashed for the door. Jones was lying on the floor with a pile of boys on top of him. An enormous woman was standing over them, grinning manically. There was nothing for it. He wouldn't hang around. He ran to the front door and out towards his car.

'Leave him to me.' Mr Watson had stayed outside with Ben and Sarah.

He sprinted towards the car and dived, as in a rugby tackle, at Sir George's legs.

It was all over.

Or nearly all over.

* * *

Taylor could see they'd won. 'OK, lads, leave him.'

The other boys stood and looked down at Jones writhing in agony on the floor.

'Right, Marrow,' there was that steely note to his voice again, 'where is she?'

'I don't know what you're talking about.' He was in a foetal position.

'If that's how you want it.' Taylor gave a signal to the other boys. They leapt forward.

'No, no, please, I'll tell you.'

'I'll take charge now.'

Taylor recognised the voice. 'Oh no', but he only whispered it.

'Hello, Sergeant. Good to see you again but I think you ought to leave this to me'

Jones couldn't believe his luck. A policeman had come to his rescue.

'Thank heavens you're here, Officer. These thugs need to be in jail.'

'Quite possibly, sir, but they're only boys. I've got a more important operation in place.' He turned towards Mr Spencer and the other masters who had all crowded into the hall. 'Drinking after hours is a serious offence ... '

'Tell me now, Marrow, or else.' Taylor realised that he had to get on.

'You'll get a really long stretch if you go on.' Jones was feeling more confident now.

'He's right, my boy.' It dawned on PC Braithwaite, however important it was to deal with the after hours drinkers, that he couldn't really stand there watching a vicious assault. 'Let him up.'

'Goodness me, Constable,' Mr Spencer was astounded by what he was witnessing. 'That's Taylor, man. He's in charge.'

'Thank you, sir,' Taylor turned back to his troops. 'Let him have it.'

'No, no,' Jones was screeching in terror, 'she's upstairs, second floor, first door on the right.'

Taylor ran to the stairs. As he reached them, he looked back at Jones.

'Is there anyone else up there?'

Jones smiled for a second, then he answered: 'No, there's no-one else here.'

'Matron,' Taylor had seen the smile, 'would you mind coming up with me? I think we may find someone else in need of that right hook.'

But Porter had heard and seen most of it. In particular, he'd seen the state of Jones' face.

'I give up.'

They all looked up and saw a trembling Jeff Porter walking downstairs, hands held above his head as if guns were trained on him.

* * *

Sam could think of nothing she could do. If only she could hear what was going on in the rest of the house, but the soundproofing was too good. All she could do was wait and hope that some opportunity would present itself.

But now there was a sound. The key was being turned. She jumped up. She would stand behind the door. Perhaps she could catch her jailer unawares and jump on him.

The door opened slowly. She held her breath. A figure appeared. She leapt.

It was only as she fell heavily on him that she realised who it was.

'Taylor,' she exclaimed.

'Watson,' he gasped. 'Funny way of saying thank you.'

* * *

Taylor would have liked to climb into a canoe, preferably with Sam, and paddle back to school but there was too much to do, and only he could do it.

First, the bumbling policeman had to be dissuaded from arresting most of the teaching staff for drinking after hours. Next, he had to be persuaded to go back to the police house and telephone for support. All the while the three villains had to be prevented from escaping.

That turned out to be not too difficult. Sir George was all too eager to get away from Mr Watson and readily agreed to go upstairs to the room in which Sam had been held, and Jones and Porter had lost any desire to fight and meekly followed.

Finally, the headmaster, the other masters and Matron had somehow to be got back to Portland Court. The boys would be no problem, they would go back in canoes, but Taylor knew there could be a disaster if he allowed the inebriated masters to attempt another crossing. Fortunately, Griffiths agreed to take a car load. The others squeezed into the Morris.

But, before they did so, Taylor took Ben aside. 'I just want to apologise, sir.'

'Apologise? Whatever for?'

'Harrogate, sir. No one else knows, sir, and no one ever will. Even if you say you're going to cane me for something I haven't done, I won't tell anyone. I had to say it earlier because of Sam, but I know it was wrong.'

'No, Taylor, it wasn't wrong. It was my fault. Never again will I doubt your word.'

* * *

They should all have been exhausted but the boys didn't seem to be tired at all. They stacked the canoes back into the boat house and walked back up to the school.

'How about raiding the kitchens for some grub?' Taylor grinned at the others. 'They're hardly going to punish us.'

His idea met with universal approval.

'I'd better go and check the Tickler's all right. I'll join you in a few minutes.'

'I'll come with you.' Tim liked the other boys but he only really felt comfortable with Taylor.

'Good for you, Crane.'

* * *

'He's ok.' Taylor was standing over the comatose body of Mr Pine, an empty sherry bottle lying by his side. 'Here, give me a hand. We'll get him onto the sofa.'

Taylor took his legs and Tim took his shoulders. He was heavy but they managed to do the job. As he lay down on the sofa, he opened his eyes.

'Taylor. It's you, isn't it?'

'It is, sir. Are you comfortable?'

'Yes, thank you. Most comfortable. But shouldn't I cane you?'

'Oh that, sir, I shouldn't worry. You can do it tomorrow, when you're feeling better.'

'Good lad. Yes, we'll leave it to the morning. Night night.' And his eyes closed again.

* * *

The midnight feast was one of the best. Taylor wished Sam was there but he understood that she would want to be at home with her father. And now, he supposed, she would go back to a girls' school. That was sad. Still, Crane was with them. He really liked Crane. It was a pity they would have to go their separate ways.

After about ten minutes they found themselves apart from the others.

'I wish you were at Portland, Crane.'

'So do I.'

'Really? After all you've seen?'

'Of course, it's a brilliant school. But my mum,' he grinned, 'I s'pose I should say my Mater, well, she couldn't afford it even if she saved up for a hundred years.'

Taylor thought for a moment and smiled. 'I've had an idea.'

* * *

The cars, Sarah's stocking still working admirably, drew up outside the main entrance. Taylor ran out, followed by the others, to greet the school staff.

One of the back doors of the black car opened. He saw a long slim leg come out. He felt his heart beating faster. It couldn't be, surely.

It was.

Sam jumped out of the car and ran to Taylor.

'Daddy told me everything on the way back. You saved my life.'

And, before he knew what was happening, he felt her lips on his cheek.

He had been kissed by a girl, and not any girl - the most beautiful girl in the country. He was glad it was dark. He could feel his face reddening. But how glorious. How wonderful. How perfect.

'Why have you come back?' he was stammering.

'This is my school and it's term time.'

'You mean you're staying?'

'Of course I am.'

Mr Spencer and Sam's father were approaching. Taylor saw that the headmaster's gait was steady. Yet again, something Taylor had noticed before, Mr Spencer had made a remarkably quick recovery from the excesses of the evening.

Tim had joined them. Now was the time to strike.

'I was just wondering, sir,' Taylor was addressing the headmaster, 'whether it might not be a good idea to give a scholarship to a deserving village boy?'

'Scholarship? No fees? What on earth are you talking about?'

Taylor sighed. Mr Spencer had sobered up too much, but he would press on.

'It's just that Crane here was an absolute brick tonight, sir. He says he'd like to come to the school but his mother can't afford the fees.'

'Goodness, I can't afford to give away free places. What an extraordinary idea.'

'Well,' Mr Watson interrupted, 'I think it's a wonderful idea. My lawyers will set it up in the morning. It will be called the "Taylor Scholarship" and the first recipient will be Tim.' He smiled at Taylor. 'Sorry, I should have called him Crane.'

* * *

Ben felt it as he walked into the house. He was being watched. Not by Mr Watson and the others standing outside. No, he was being watched from somewhere else and by someone he didn't know. He had almost told Sarah about the watcher just before Pine had burst into the common room proclaiming his intention of caning Taylor and Crane. In a way, he was glad he had been stopped. Sarah seemed to understand everything but even she might have had some difficulty in accepting the theory of the watcher.

But he had to tell someone. He would be driven mad by it if he didn't.

He turned back to the front door. Taylor, grinning widely at the success of the scholarship plan, was making his way into the house.

How idiotic he had been. Of course, there was only one person he could explain it to. Even if Taylor thought him insane, the boy would never tell anyone else and, if there was anyone at Portland Court who could discover the truth, that person was Taylor.

'Sir,' the boy was almost jumping with delight, 'did you hear, sir? Crane's coming to Portland Court, on a scholarship.'

'Yes, I heard. That's wonderful news.'

'Are you all right, sir?'

'Yes, of course.'

Taylor came closer to him. 'It's just, well, it's just ... you look a bit worried, sir.'

Ben looked out to the drive. The others were all still there. He made a sudden decision.

'Can we have a word, Taylor, in the masters' common room?'

Taylor frowned. 'Have I done something wrong, sir?'

'Goodness me, no, I'd just value your advice about something. Would you mind?'

'Of course not, sir.'

Ben led the boy into the common room.

'Oh, blast,' he had seen Mr Pine. 'We'd better find somewhere else.'

'Don't worry about him, sir. He won't wake up for a few hours yet.' Taylor closed the door. 'We may not have much time, sir. The other masters will probably need a night cap.'

Although Ben had firmly resolved to tell Taylor, he had some difficulty in finding the words.

Taylor came to the rescue.

'Do you sometimes get the feeling you're being watched, sir?'

Ben stared, open-mouthed, at the twelve year old.

'What did you just say, Taylor?'

'I just thought you might, occasionally, have a sort of sensation of being spied on, sir.'

Ben couldn't speak but he managed to nod.

'I've been wondering about it, sir, for quite a time. I've got some ideas. Maybe it'd be better not to tell anyone else about it quite yet.'

Ben found his voice again. 'Yes, I'm sure you're right, Taylor.' He managed a weak smile. 'We wouldn't want everyone thinking I'd gone the round the bend.'

'Oh, sir, I didn't mean that. It's just that I think it'll be easier to work out what's going on if only you and I know about it.' He thought for a moment. 'Well,' he added, 'perhaps we should bring Watson and Crane in on it. I think we make quite a good team.

There's certainly something very strange going on here. I'm sure someone's watching and, whoever it is, is watching you. There has to be a reason.'

They heard the sound of several footsteps in the hall.

'Can we talk tomorrow, sir? We could meet here, half an hour before breakfast. The other masters are bound to have a bit of a lie in.'

Ben glanced in the direction of Mr Pine.

'Don't worry, sir, he can't be very comfortable. He'll wake up before dawn and he'll go to his room. He won't want to risk being found here.'

'Very well, tomorrow morning.'

The door opened. Mr Spencer, followed by the other masters, came in.

'Ah, Glossop, there you are. I wonder if you'd mind settling the boys down for the night. The rest of us have had quite a strenuous time and I think we deserve a bit of a rest.' As he spoke, Mr Spencer spotted Taylor. 'Goodness, boy, what are you doing here? You should be in bed.'

Taylor gave an almost imperceptible wink to Ben. 'Yes, sir. I just thought I'd better see whether Mr Pine wanted to cane me but he seems to have nodded off.'

'What nonsense. Of course he won't cane you.'

'I expect you're right, sir, but I did give him my word. Anyway, I'll go to bed now, sir.' He turned to leave, then looked back at his headmaster. 'I hope you don't think I'm being patronising, sir, but I thought you and the other masters were really brilliant tonight. We'd never have rescued Watson if you hadn't turned up.'

Mr Spencer coughed modestly. 'All in the line of duty, Taylor. Off you go now.'

* * *

Taylor insisted on escorting Sam up to her room.

He didn't hold out much hope but there might just be a chance that that glorious kiss would be repeated.

They reached her door.

'Quite a day really.' Did that sound silly? Probably, but he felt rather silly, almost as if he had been drinking sherry from the masters' common room.

'It was.' She smiled at him. 'And there's more to come.'

He frowned. What did she mean?

'I'll tell you in the morning. But I'm sure there's something odd here at Portland.'

'What do you mean?'

She held up her hand. 'I'm tired. Wait till the morning. Now, am I allowed another kiss?'

THE END

Lightning Source UK Ltd.
Milton Keynes UK
UKOW020709050112

184781UK00004B/8/P

9 781613 648377